Slave Girl

Slave Girl

Original title: Cowslip

by BETSY HAYNES

Cover Illustration by Moneta Barnett

SCHOLASTIC · BOOK SERVICES

NEW YORK · TORONTO · LONDON · AUCKLAND · SYDNEY · TOKYO

ISBN: 0-590-06119-4

Copyright © 1973 by Betsy Haynes. This edition is published by Scholastic Book Services, a division of Scholastic Magazines, Inc., by arrangement with Thomas Nelson, Inc., publishers of the book under the title COWSLIP.

14 13 12 11 10 9 8 7 6 5   9/7 01/8

Printed in the U.S.A.

Slave Girl

CHAPTER 1

The yellow bandanna was the only special thing that Cowslip ever owned. She spread it across her lap, gently smoothing out the wrinkles with her small brown hand, and blinked back the tears that welled up in her eyes. Then she stared as hard as she could into her lap, trying to see only the beautiful bandanna instead of the crowded slave market all around her.

If only she could make the horrible reality of the slave pen disappear by refusing to look at it. But she knew that she could not, so after a moment she tied the bandanna over her hair and gathered the other children near. The coffle was made up of eleven slave children, bound together by coarse ropes, and they huddled close to Cowslip, peering around like frightened mice. She was afraid, too, but she was thirteen and the oldest and she could not let it show.

The pen they were in usually held stock and it stank like a barn lot. Now half a dozen gangs of slaves packed one end. They crouched, owl-eyed and silent, watching workmen at the other end of the pen put the last touches on the makeshift platform upon which they would soon be paraded to be sold.

Gentlemen buyers in tall hats and swallow-tail coats milled around in front of the platform like flocks of big birds while they waited for the bidding to start. Some talked among themselves, laughing and going on as if they were at a church social. Others strutted about, looking over the coffles of slaves that would soon be put on the block and stopping now and then to examine a slave or haggle a bit with a trader before moving on.

Which one of these men would pay cash money for her and lead her off to Lord knows what? Cowslip wondered.

But first, she would have to stand up there on that auction block in front of everybody. What if her legs turned to molasses and would not hold her up? What would they do to her then? Cowslip shuddered and tried to rub away the goose bumps on her arms.

There was a commotion near the gate. It swung open and a tall spindly man, wearing a drooping moustache and carrying a gold-handled cane, hurried into the pen. The crowd parted for him as he strode toward the platform. Quickly mounting the steps, he rapped his cane on the floor as a signal for quiet.

"Gentlemen! May I have your attention, please?" he said loudly. "Daniel R. Crimmins, at your service. I have just arrived here in your fair city of Columbus, Kentucky, this twenty-ninth day of June, eighteen hundred sixty-one, to offer you a choice lot of Negroes consisting of plantation hands, carpenters, blacksmiths, cooks, laundresses, and what have you."

While the auctioneer went on and on about the fine quality of the slaves and marveled at the good fortune of the buyers to be present at his sale that day, Cowslip watched one of the traders arrange his slaves on the platform. He pushed the young, strong ones to the front and stripped field hands to the waist to show off their rippling muscles. When he had them displayed like goods on a peddler's cart, the bidding began.

"Heynow, whatdoIhear, whatdoIhear? Who'llgivemeathousanddollars, thousanddollars, thousanddollars, who'llgivemeathousanddollars?"

The children fidgeted nervously as the auctioneer's voice droned on.

"I don't want to go up there," Flossie whimpered, locking her arms around Cowslip's neck. "I'm scared."

"I know," Cowslip answered gently. "But it will all be over in a whipstitch. Then everything will be all right again. You'll see."

"No, it won't." Amos shook his head. His sorrowful black eyes were brimming with tears. "They'll sell us apart. I know they will."

"Sh," she said. "You mustn't talk like that."

Cowslip glanced fearfully toward the auction block. The first gang of slaves was being sold fast, and soon only one remained, an old man long past his prime. The auctioneer tried frantically to draw a bid, waving his cane with one hand and a fistful of dollar bills with the other as he chanted. No one wanted the old slave, and finally Cowslip saw the auctioneer motion him off the platform. His trader, a short-legged man who was as scrunched up and ugly as the devil's own doll baby, was waiting below, and he grabbed the old man and set him to dancing squarely in front of the platform.

"Look happy," the trader ordered.

The old man managed a wooden grin, but tears began to stream down his face.

Cowslip swallowed hard.

"I·got to put my scaredness under my feet and stand on it," she told herself firmly. "The young'uns is counting on me."

Cowslip set her mouth in a firm straight line and closed her eyes for a moment. When she opened them again, she did it slowly and deliberately as if she were opening her former master's fancy curtains and peering out at the quiet cotton fields, where the rows stretched on like long green fingers for as far as a person could see.

It was there that Mariah had always said, "The first thing a slave's got to learn is never to let no white folks know he's scared. Your face got to be as blank as if you was dead."

Mariah was the old black woman in charge of the childhouse on the Missouri plantation that Cowslip had come from. It was Mariah's job to tend the slave children so that their mothers would not have to take time from their work to feed and care for them. Cowslip did not remember her own mother. Mariah said she had died when Cowslip was born.

Mariah saw to it that the children under her charge had all manner of things that Master would not have allowed if he had known about them — things like warm horse blankets, which she stole from the barn and hid in the potato hole under the cabin floor during the day. She had even tried to sneak meat out of the smokehouse for them, but Master had caught her and told her that as a punishment he would cut the food ration for the childhouse in half for a month to teach her a lesson. It was then that Mariah had decided to cast her spell.

Mariah knew all about black magic. She used to gather the children around her after supper, when the light from the fireplace had softened to a glow, and tell them stories about the strange and secret powers black folks possessed. She said that blacks knew spells and curses so powerful that masters could not fight them off, though they might be armed with whips and chains.

The children always begged to see Mariah work her magic.

"Oh, no," she would say. "The laying on of spells and curses is a terrible serious thing, never to be done just for fun. Besides, it's got to be done in the middle of the night, long past the time that young'uns is asleep."

Sometimes the children would play possum, trying to stay awake and spy, but sleep always snatched them away before the hoodoo began.

Then one night Cowslip was awakened from a midnight sleep by the sound of her name. It had come like the crackle of dry twigs set aflame, like the scratch of branches against the cabin wall, but it had been her name. She was sure of that.

"Don't be scared," a hoarse voice whispered. Cowslip shuddered and slowly opened her eyes. It was only Mariah. She was sitting in a patch of moonlight on the cabin floor, holding something in her cupped hands.

It was too dark for Cowslip to see what Mariah was doing. "You laying on a curse?" she asked, as she slipped quietly to the old woman's side.

Mariah nodded somberly. "Time you commenced to learn black magic," she said. "I'm getting mighty old. The day is coming when you'll have to carry on."

"Glory be!" Cowslip whispered excitedly. "You suppose I got the brains?"

The old lady chuckled softly and motioned for her to come nearer. Cowslip bent close to see what was in her hands. It was a dead bird. Mariah gently laid it in Cowslip's lap and picked up a scrap of paper off the floor. She wadded the paper into a ball the size of a pea and stuffed it into the bird's mouth.

"That paper's got Master's name wrote

down on it," she said. "And when this here bird dries up, you watch for troubles and misfortunes to shower down on him like leaves in an autumn windstorm. I reckon that will pay him back for the mean and spiteful thing he's doing to all my young'uns."

Before Mariah went to bed, she told Cowslip to hide the bird under a bush near the childhouse where she could check it every day. Cowslip lay awake for a long time after that. Thoughts of the curse and of Mariah who loved all the children as if they were her own spun around inside her head like a weather vane.

As time passed, Cowslip kept checking the dead bird. Slowly it dried up. At the same time the leaves of the young cotton plants slowly became yellow between their veins. Then the roots and stems turned black.

"Black rot," Mariah said with a satisfied smile. It was one of the diseases cotton planters dreaded most, and Mariah was sure her children's misery was being revenged by the spell she had cast.

The disease had come early enough in the season for Master to replant the cotton crop, but he was forced to borrow money to buy the seed. Then, two days before the first installment on his loan was due, he announced that some of the slaves would have to be sold so he could make the payment.

He would sell everyone in the childhouse over the age of four first, he said, even though they would not bring much, because he needed all of the bigger slaves to get the second crop of cotton into the ground. Mariah's curse, which had seemed so glorious at first, had surely come to a sorrowful end.

On the day the children were led away by a slave trader named Rueben Baxter, Mariah slipped the yellow bandanna into Cowslip's hand. She sent something with each one of the children — a scrap of cloth, a few bright beads, a chipped dish — and with each went the memory of love.

Mariah kept her own face blank when she handed out her treasures and said good-bye to the children under the stern gaze of the speculator. But Cowslip knew that deep inside she must be crying, because as surely as a raincrow's holler brings rain, it was Mariah's spell of black magic that had caused them to be sold.

Baxter, the trader, had marched the children off down the road fastened together by a rope that was fitted around their necks like a halter. Riding behind them on his horse, he cracked his whip over their heads whenever they slowed down, and muttered loudly about a wasted trip and a pack of worthless brats.

Late in the afternoon they reached the Mississippi River. Cowslip had heard about the river often, but she had never seen it before, and she watched in wonder as it coasted lazily between its widespread banks, ripples lapping softly against the shore like little cat tongues. At the landing, Baxter herded them aboard a flatboat, and they grabbed for the railing at the first shock of water slipping away beneath them. The boat drifted downriver for a bit and then headed across the muddy waters, docking at Columbus.

They had spent the night on the cold, hard ground of the slave pen. There were other gangs of slaves scattered here and there, some of them with children among them, but nowhere was there another coffle made up entirely of young'uns. The other slaves stared at them in sad disbelief.

After a while, deep measured sounds of sleep mingled with stifled sobs. Cowslip had meant to stay watchful all through the night, but her body ached for rest. Little by little her eyelids drooped until she, too, fell into a fitful sleep, from which she roused every once in a while to reach out a protective hand over the cluster of children around her and stroke away a bad dream.

Shortly before dawn she was awakened when three traders entered the pen. One of them was carrying a lantern, which he placed on a table in a far corner.

Cowslip held her breath as they sorted through the gangs of slaves, unlocking one here and another there, and leading them to the lighted corner. She crouched low and pretended to be asleep each time a trader came near.

No one bothered her. Instead they chose old men and women who looked as if they were barely able to work. The traders rubbed oil on wrinkled skin until it shone and bootblack into graying heads of hair, and yanked white hairs out of the stubble on quivering chins. After a while, the group of old slaves looked young and fit enough for almost any kind of work.

Glory be, thought Cowslip. Some master is going to pay a passel for one of them, and all he'll get for his money is a bag of tired old bones.

Morning finally came, and the traders passed out batches of ash cake and salt pork. With breakfast over, there had been nothing to do but wait.

Now that the auction had begun, the children scooted around restlessly on the dirt floor and the old man danced on and on in front of the platform, still smiling and still crying while his sweat-soaked clothes clung to him.

Something warm splattered against Cowslip's leg. Startled, she looked down at a wet wad of tobacco that had landed only inches from where she sat. Her stomach knotted with fear. A buyer stood nearby and he was regarding her thoughtfully.

Tobacco juice trickled through his beard and made a brown stain on the pale-green waistcoat that strained to cover his stomach. He was short and squat and his mouth seemed to stretch from one ear to the other.

"Scared you, did I, girl?"

Cowslip's heart beat wildly as the man started toward her.

CHAPTER 2

Cowslip managed to keep her face blank even though her heart beat against her chest like a loose shutter in a gale.

"You trained for looking after children?" the man asked.

"I ain't trained for nothing," she said in a shaking voice.

The man bit off a hunk of tobacco and settled into a slouch, chewing slowly and looking at her as if she were a piece of spoiled fish. If only he would go away, she thought. She clasped her hands in her lap, so he would not see them trembling, and stared at the ground.

Baxter had left his slaves alone most of the

morning, but now he seemed to appear from nowhere, smiling broadly at the buyer.

"Rueben Baxter's the name," he said, extending his hand.

"Colonel Thaddeus Sprague," the man said coldly. He ignored Baxter's outstretched hand and pointed toward Cowslip. "Does she belong to you?"

"Yes, sirree, and she's a fine slave too," Baxter said, roughly pulling Cowslip to her feet. "She eats next to nothing and can do the work of three."

The buyer answered with a grunt and began poking and prodding at Cowslip's bony frame. He pulled her jaws apart and peered into her mouth as if he were inspecting a horse. His warm sour breath was smothering, and she ached to sink her teeth into his fingers. Instead, she stood motionless, staring right through him as she would stare through a window, knowing that drawing even one drop of a white man's blood meant death for a black. It was the law.

"How old are you, girl?" Colonel Sprague asked.

"She's thirteen, according to her papers," said Baxter before Cowslip could speak. Then he added hastily, "She may be small for her age, but she's not frail. No, sir!"

"Let me see you walk," the Colonel said. Cowslip paced back and forth as far as her ropes would allow until he held up his hand for her to stop.

"Well, at least she isn't lame," he muttered. "How much would you take for her?"

"Eight hundred dollars, and that's a bargain," said Baxter, stomping around nervously.

Colonel Sprague sighed heavily and slowly looked her over again. Cowslip winced. Was this the moment she had been dreading? She felt the children pressing around her as if they were trying to keep her from being taken away.

"I'll give you six hundred," said the Colonel.

"Six hundred!" Baxter roared. "Why, think of all the years of work she's got in her. No, I couldn't let her go for six hundred. Eight hundred dollars. And that's a bargain."

"I'll wait for the bidding," the Colonel said with a frown. He turned and walked away.

Baxter started to go after him, then changed his mind and stomped off in the direction of a group of traders standing near the platform.

Cowslip's knees felt limp as she sank back to the ground. The children snuggled close, piling into her lap like eager pups, and they hugged each other in silent joy. The danger had passed, at least for a little while.

Another gang of slaves was on the platform, big, strapping field hands, and the bidding was getting heated.

Who in tarnation is ever going to want a mess of young'uns? Cowslip wondered.

It was true that slave children were expected to do their share of work, but what could they do that would make them worth buying? The little ones were only quarter hands and could just do things like pulling weeds or cleaning the yard or picking cotton. As slave children got older their jobs got harder, and they went from quarter hands to half hands, and then to three-quarter hands. Finally, when they got to be eighteen or nineteen, they became full hands.

Cowslip had been half a hand on the old plantation. She had helped Mariah look after the childhouse. She had helped the dairy maid with the churning and chopped cotton in the fields and done odd jobs around the big house. Sometimes she carried water to the field hands in heavy wooden buckets, while Lycergus straggled along behind her toting the gourd dippers. Lycergus had the longest name and the shortest legs of any of the plantation young'uns, and he always trailed behind like a catbird's tail.

"I got to stop dwelling on how things used

to be," Cowslip thought, and she reached out and stroked Lycergus' soft woolly head.

Two more gangs of slaves were auctioned off, and then the dreaded moment had come. Using the butt of his whip, Baxter prodded Cowslip and the children to their feet. He removed the rope halter from around their necks and hustled them toward the platform.

"Get on up there," he growled when they reached the steps.

Cowslip could scarcely hear the noisy confusion of the slave market above the pounding of her heart. The children stood behind her, waiting for her to make a move. She had to lead them up there like little lambs to slaughter, she thought. Slowly she climbed the stairs and they followed.

"Come on, come on," the auctioneer urged impatiently.

Baxter pushed his way through the children and jerked Cowslip by the arm, leading her to the center of the platform. Then he lined the children in a row behind her.

Cowslip looked out over the slave pen. She had never seen so many faces in one place in all her life. It reminded her of a whole field full of ripe cotton bolls bobbing in the breeze. The auctioneer glanced over a sheet of paper that Baxter had given him and then called for silence. The heads stopped bobbing, the pen grew quiet, and all eyes turned toward Cowslip.

The auctioneer leaned on his cane, slowly looking her up and down. He circled her once and then addressed the buyers.

"I have here a girl of exceptional quality, thirteen years old, sound of limb and strong of back. She's young enough to train for domestic duty and old enough to give a good day's work. Gentlemen, what will you bid?"

Cowslip closed her eyes. She could not look at all those faces, all those eyes, examining her as if she were a piece of yard goods or a sack of flour.

It will all be over in a whipstitch. That was what she had told Flossie, and she had to believe it too.

"Five hundred dollars," someone shouted from the crowd.

"Fivehundreddollars, fivehundreddollars. DoIhearsix, who'llgivemesix, givemesixgivemesix?"

Try as she would, Cowslip could not shut out the sound of the auctioneer's voice. His singsong went on and on as he tried to coax a higher bid.

"Sixhundreddollars, sixhundreddollars. Who'llgivemesixhundreddollars?"

The buyers began to shuffle around restlessly, and the hum of their conversation rose little by little.

"Going once for five hundred dollars," the auctioneer said at last. "Going twice. Sold for five hundred dollars!"

It was over. She was sold. Behind her, Cowslip heard one of the children begin to sniffle. She longed to turn around and hug each one of them and tell them good-bye, but she did not dare. Instead, she swallowed hard, trying to get rid of the lump that filled her throat. A numbness spread through her body, and her arms and legs felt almost as if they were floating as she slowly walked back down the steps to face a new life with a new master.

Colonel Sprague pushed his way through the crowd. She had been sure it would be him. He counted the bills out of a roll into the auctioneer's waiting hand and then turned to Cowslip.

"What's your name, girl?" he asked. He stuffed her papers into a pocket in one of the tails of his coat and bit off another chew of tobacco.

The only part of Cowslip that was not trembling was her face, and she had to grit her teeth to keep it still.

"Cowslip," she said, digging a big toe into the dirt.

"Cowslip?" he said, as if he had not heard her right. Her old master had named her because her mother had died when she was born, and he always picked names for the motherless slave babies that sounded like mean jokes, names like Hungry and Liability and Hog Jaw and Cowslip.

"Well, if that's not a good one," Colonel Sprague said with a chuckle. "Come along then, Cowslip. Let's go."

He led her to a blacksmith just outside the slave pen. He was a giant of a white man with a bald head and a gold ring made to look like a snake coiled around one of his fingers, and he was forging irons for newly purchased gangs of slaves. Here and there, groups of slaveowners stood around talking while they waited.

"Add this girl to those ten field hands over there," Colonel Sprague instructed the blacksmith. "I have business in town. I'll be back for them in a little while."

The blacksmith nodded and bellowed up the fire, barely glancing at Cowslip.

"Nothing in my life will ever be the same," she thought as she stared into the blacksmith's fire. "I ain't never going to see Mariah or none of them young'uns again."

Cowslip had never been away from home

before, because a slave had to carry a piece of paper written by his master saying that it was all right for him to leave the plantation. The note would say who he was, where he was going, and when he was supposed to be back home, and a slave was almost never allowed to stay away overnight. It took a mighty important reason for a master to write a note like that.

Outside the slave market where she stood, the townspeople were going about their noonday chores in a world that was far different from the slow life on the plantation. Slowly the strange new sights and sounds began seeping in around the edges of Cowslip's thoughts. She could not shut out the noises of the heavy wagons rattling over the cobblestones or the draymen whipping their horses and shouting greetings to each other when they passed or the street peddlers hawking their wares.

Down the street a woman dipped a broom into a bucket of sudsy water and scrubbed the dirt off her front stoop. Absently, Cowslip watched the water trickle away in little rivers down the side of the street.

Suddenly she was aware of something even stranger than all these new sights.

No one was holding on to her. She was not chained. In fact, none of the people standing nearby were paying the smallest bit of attention to the slave girl in the yellow bandanna. She stood alone, able to walk away without even a note and lose herself in the crowded street.

She might never get another chance. The blacksmith was busy fitting a neck iron to a young woman who kept a protective hand over the baby on her hip. He would not see her go. Long lines of slaves, chained to each other and then to stakes driven into the ground, gazed mostly at their feet while they waited for their new masters to lead them away. The buyers were keeping watch over them out of the corners of their eyes, but Colonel Sprague was nowhere in sight. For the first time in her life, Cowslip was free.

CHAPTER 3

"I got to run," she thought. "Because any minute somebody's going to see me. They're going to say, 'Slave girl, where's your chains?' Then I won't be free no more."

It was only a few steps to the crowded street where both blacks and whites hurried by. If she could get that far, she could very likely pass for a town slave off on an errand for her mistress. Or maybe she could hide somewhere, in a barn perhaps, until dark, and then slip away unseen. If no one stopped her, she could just keep right on going. Somewhere. But where?

North, of course. Mariah had said that moss always grew on the north sides of trees. She would find her way north by that. Then, when she got there, she would spend her time just walking around. She would walk around and walk around until she got plain tired of going where she pleased when she pleased and of doing what she pleased, like white folks.

The blacksmith turned away from her now, and no one else seemed to notice that she was there. It was the perfect time to run. Slowly she inched one foot a short way in the dirt, but the other one refused to follow.

"Suppose I get away and head up north," she thought, "what'll I do then? How'll I stay alive until I get there? I ain't got enough brains. I ain't never lived off roots and berries. I'm too plain dumb to tell the poison from the good. I ain't never caught a rabbit or found water fit to drink." Her forehead wrinkled in a frown. "Like Old Master said, us blacks is too ignorant to do for ourselves, so we got to be took care of."

Cowslip shuddered as she watched the blacksmith lift the blood-red metal out of the fire with a long pair of tongs and pound it into a link for a chain. "I'll be took care of, all right.

I'll be wearing chains and feeling whips for the rest of my days if I don't get away right now," she said to herself.

She scratched her head and tried to conjure up a picture of a forest in her mind. All she could see were towering trees and shadowy tangles of underbrush where danger might lurk and slave catchers could lie in wait. She thought about the slaves she had known on the old plantation who had tried to run away. They had been full-grown men who knew a lot more about everything than she did, but they had all been caught. Some of them had claimed to know forty-eleven ways to outfox a slave catcher, but the white slave catchers must have known forty-twelve ways of tracking slaves. When the slave catchers brought the runaways back, Old Master called them an ignorant pack of fools and had them whipped.

After that a preacher had started coming to the plantation to hold church just for the slaves. That preacher said it was the curse of Noah that blacks would always be slaves, no matter what they did. He even read it right out of the Bible.

The preacher told that story every time he came, so it was easy to remember. He said that after the great flood, Noah set to work again and planted himself a vineyard. The grapes from the vineyard were made into wine. One day Noah drank too much of the wine and fell asleep in his tent without any clothes on.

Noah's son Ham walked in and saw his father sleeping there naked and told his two brothers Shem and Japheth. Then they brought a piece of cloth and covered him up, walking in backward so they would not look at him.

When Noah woke up, he figured out what Ham had done, and he got so mad he set a curse on Ham's boy Canaan that he would always be a slave. The preacher said all blacks came down from Ham. If that was so, there was no use to run away. She would always be a slave. It was the will of the Lord.

One thing that Cowslip never could figure out, though, was why Noah had punished Canaan for something he didn't even do.

"I guess blacks ain't smart enough to understand," she thought.

"Cowslip!"

The word cut into her thoughts like the lash of a whip. Her chance was gone. Colonel Sprague was back.

"Come along," he called. "I've got to get you fastened on so we can start for home."

"It's the will of the Lord," Cowslip told herself sternly. "Besides, what's the good of being free, anyway, if you're cold and hungry and you got no place to go and no one to share your misery with? If I can just do what Colonel Sprague tells me to do and not get into any kind of trouble, everything'll be fine."

Cowslip cringed as the blacksmith placed his enormous hands with its snake ring on her neck and brought the tips of his fingers together in back. Then he lumbered to the far wall of his shop, where neck irons of every size hung on pegs. When he had chosen one, he added a length of chain, pounding together the fastening link with blows that shook the ground beneath her feet. His bare chest was shiny with sweat, and Cowslip watched the reflected flames from the fire leap across his skin.

At last he motioned that the neck iron was ready. Cowslip followed him to the line of field hands, clenched her fists as tightly as she could, and closed her eyes.

Like the strike of a snake, there was a sudden shock of cold metal and then a heaviness that pushed so hard against her shoulders that she could hardly stand up. Her heart was heavy too. It was settled now. She would remain a slave.

As soon as she was shackled on behind the other slaves, Colonel Sprague mounted his horse and signaled for them to march. The long queue shuffled slowly through the town, attracting attention on every street. Dogs barked, small boys made jeering faces, and people stopped their chatting to stare. Cowslip was glad when they finally reached the quiet countryside and followed a road that led between rust-colored fields dotted green by tobacco plants.

She had never worn chains before, and after a while her neck was raw from the rubbing of the heavy iron. They trudged along the road for what seemed like forever before the Colonel signaled for them to turn onto a treelined lane. The branches came together and touched overhead, making Cowslip feel as though she were walking through a lacy tunnel.

The lane ended at a gate, and a tall lank man leaned against it. The butt of a whip was stuck inside his belt.

Must be the overseer, Cowslip thought.

The man swung the gate open, and the Colonel rode through, calling over his shoulder as he went by, "They're all yours, Tanner."

"Come along now and get your rations," Tanner ordered.

The field hands mumbled among themselves as they followed the overseer, not paying any attention to the solitary young girl who trailed behind them. Cowslip did not mind. This was her new home, where she might spend the rest of her days, and her head jerked from one side to the other as she tried to see it all at once.

From the gate the road led between two pastures where tall horses with coats like brown velvet munched on the lush grass. Beyond the pasture, on the left side of the road, were tobacco fields as far as Cowslip could see, and the pasture on the right side was bordered by a stand of timber.

After a while the road turned abruptly to the right and cut straight through the timber. When the slaves came out the other side, there, towering over them from the crest of a sweeping hill, was the big house. Cowslip looked at it in wonder. It was twice as big as the house on the old plantation. It was made of dark-red brick and was three floors high. There were two porches, one on the ground floor and one above it, which reached all the way across the house. Each porch was lined with tall white pillars.

Like rows of teeth in a smiling mouth, Cowslip thought. She chuckled to herself. "Why, if that house don't look like a grinning slave, I never saw one. But I bet Colonel Sprague don't see it that way."

Tanner led them across the wide, well-kept

lawn and Cowslip saw that behind the big house, draped softly like a shawl around the shoulder of land belonging to her new master, was the Mississippi River. Two long lines of slave cabins trailed off down the hill behind the big house like pigtail braids. They were deserted at this time of day, and sat, like forgotten mud pies, baking in the late afternoon sun. About midway down and stuck off at some distance to one side was a building that was twice the size of the slave cabins. Tanner headed straight for it.

He unlocked the padlocked door and pushed it open, motioning for them to follow him inside. Cowslip looked around the stuffy room. The walls were lined with boxes and barrels and sacks that looked as if they held meal or grain. In one corner, covered with a jumble of papers, was Tanner's desk. Through an open doorway Cowslip could see his living quarters, a single room with a rumpled bed and clothes strewn around the floor.

Tanner unchained them, unlocking each neck iron as he passed down the line of slaves. His movements were slow and loose, and Cowslip closed her eyes when he came to her.

"He's like a snake just woke up from sleeping in the sun," she mused. Nevertheless, she was happy to be rid of the terrible neck iron, and she rubbed her sore flesh in relief.

Tanner began doling out the food rations, putting each slave's share into a long tow sack. In each sack he dropped a bushel bag of Indian meal, a pint of salt, and two pounds of smoked fish.

"The meal and salt have got to last you for a month," he said. "The fish is for a week."

He went down the line filling sacks until he came to Cowslip. Then he stopped.

"None for you," he growled, and turned away.

Cowslip could not believe what she had heard. What would she eat? Surely he did not mean for her to starve.

She was too afraid to speak, so she watched in silence as he handed out clothing to the field hands. Tanner told them that this was all they would get for a year, and he carefully subtracted what they were wearing from the clothes that they were entitled to get.

Again Tanner passed her by as he gave out one blanket, one jacket, one pair of heavy brogue shoes, two shirts, and two pairs of trousers to each of the field hands.

Finally, he motioned Cowslip to the door. "Go up to the big house," he said. "Job will tell you what to do."

The big house! she thought.

Her heart was hummingbird fluttery as she hurried up the hill. Where would she be now if she had taken the chance to run away from the slave market? Hungry, alone, afraid, maybe even dead. Instead, she was on her way to the big house, probably to be trained for a high position like cook or laundress or maid. Maybe Colonel Sprague would let her mind the children, since that was what he had asked her about back at the slave market.

Cowslip supposed that she would start out as a helper, but even that was far above the work of the field hands. If it was the will of the Lord that blacks be slaves, He surely was smiling on her now. She would get a pretty dress, maybe a bright-colored calico. And shoes — she would have her very first pair of shoes!

Slave children were never given shoes until they were old enough to become full hands or have a fine job in the big house. They learned early how to prod hogs out of their wallowing places and stick their cold feet down into the mud to warm them, or how to nestle them in the ashes of the fireplace after the flames had dwindled away.

Cowslip looked back at the tobacco fields,

where gangs of slaves were hard at work with their hoes.

"Could be I'm turning my back forever on them fields," she thought. "Glory be!"

The back door to the big house stood ajar. Cowslip's heart pounded as she tiptoed into the kitchen, where the hot, stuffy air was filled with a mixture of delicious smells. A table in the center of the room was covered with dirty dishes, silverware, and cups, and Cowslip's mouth watered at the sight of discarded crusts and scraps of food.

"Mercy me, you're finally here!"

Before Cowslip could look around to see who was talking to her, a huge black woman with blobs of flour on her face and arms grabbed her around the waist and propelled her straight toward a door on the other side of the room.

"Mistress been looking for you since morning, and she's nearly broke out in fits."

"But where's Job?" Cowslip insisted. "The overseer said I was to see Job."

"Don't you never mind about Job now," the woman answered. She was puffing and panting, but she kept going full speed until she reached the door. "Mistress will tell you when you can see him. Right now, you go on down this hall as fast as you can and clean to the top of the stairs. The door at the end is where Mistress be. Now shoo!"

Cowslip started off down the hall at a run. She could see the shadow of the winding staircase ahead, and she made a leaping turn just as she got there.

She had no idea where the man had come from who stood on the bottom step, but there he was. Jerking herself sideways, she sat down hard and narrowly missed barreling into him.

CHAPTER 4

The man who stood on the stair calmly looking down at her was just about the grandest-
looking black man that Cowslip had ever seen.
He had to be the butler in all those fancy
clothes. He wore black pants and a dark-red
coat, and his shirt and gloves were whiter than
the stars. But it was not his clothes that made
him look so grand. Cowslip had seen butlers
before, and some of them were fancier. Maybe
it was the straight way he stood or the quiet
look in his eyes. Whatever it was about him,
she did not have time to think about it now.

She scrambled to her feet and tried to slip past him. He had not moved even so much as a hair.

"I got to go," she said frantically. "Mistress been looking for me since morning."

He put out a hand to stop her. "It's all right, girl," he said in a voice as quiet as his eyes. "Mistress won't be needing you until tomorrow."

"Oh," she whispered, secretly hoping that Mistress would be in a better mood by then.

"I'm Job," he said. "And I suppose you're the new girl who's going to tend the children while Mistress is away."

"I guess so," Cowslip said hopefully. "I'm the only girl he bought, and the driver sent me looking for you."

"What's your name?"

"Cowslip," she said, almost in a whisper.

"Cowslip?" He raised his eyebrows in surprise. Then, after a pause, he added, "So that's what you are?"

"*What* I am! What you mean by that?" She was beginning to dislike this strange slave who talked more like a white man than a black.

"A cowslip," he began, gazing off somewhere over her head and talking as if he were remembering something from a long time ago. "A yellow flower that grows wild and free with nothing to do all day but warm itself in the sun and drink the sweet rain. My, my. Aren't you lucky to have a name like that!"

Cowslip stared at him. Her name usually made people laugh, not think of something pretty.

"Well, Cowslip," he said. The name sounded different when he said it. "You go on down to the white cabin for tonight. I'll be waiting for you in the morning, so don't dally on the way. We've got to get you started off right with Mistress."

Cowslip hurried out of the house, tiptoeing through the kitchen so that the cook would not see her and send her racing off somewhere again. Job had said to go to the white cabin. Cowslip's heart fluttered at the thought.

The white cabin was always the one where the unmarried female house slaves lived. It was always nearer to the big house than the other cabins, so that Master and Mistress could easily call the slaves to work, even in the dead of night, if they wanted to, and it was white-washed so it would not spoil the looks of the big house.

On the way down the hill she could not keep from thinking about Job. What made him so different? He was a slave, but he did not act like one. Where did he get that strange way of talking? There was something almost scary in his quiet ways.

It was nearly dark, and in the distance she could see the field hands filing slowly around the finger of timber and along the outer edges of the tobacco fields, like long lines of ants. Men and women, young and old, they had been laboring since daybreak, and now they trudged silently toward the cabins.

She stopped to watch, staying far enough in the shadows to keep from being seen.

As they came near, a wave of homesickness blinded her with tears. She rubbed the tears away and then gasped, looking closer at the slaves. Why, she knew them — they were her friends. But why couldn't she fit names to their faces?

Then, just as suddenly as she had known them, they became strangers again. "Guess after a day's work in the fields all that's left of a body is tiredness and scaredness, and one plantation's slaves look like all the others," she thought sadly.

Back on the old plantation, Mariah would be feeding the young'uns their supper right about now. There would be precious little in their bowls to eat, so they would fill themselves with playful laughter and with Mariah's long-winded yarns.

After supper, when the fire had burned down low, the little ones would scamper off to bed. In the old days, Cowslip had always stayed up to help Mariah make ash cakes for the next day. Side by side, they would mix a little water with cornmeal until their spoons could stand up straight in it. Then they would wrap the dough in fresh oak leaves and bury it in the hot ashes in the fireplace. The cakes would cook slowly and be ready to eat the next morning.

"Glory be," Cowslip thought. "I wonder where all them young'uns is tonight?"

"Why, girl, how come you is standing out here all by yourself?"

Cowslip whirled around and came face to face with the cook, who looked at her solemnly. In the light of the rising moon the woman's solid frame cast a shadow that stretched off down the hillside as wide as a house.

"I — I was j-j-just . . ."

"I didn't mean to scare you none," said the cook. The look in her eyes softened. "You all right?"

Cowslip nodded.

"I'm Mehitabel. You come on down to the cabin now and settle in."

"My name's Cowslip. Job says it means a flower that's wild and free."

"Well, Job would most likely know," said Mehitabel, leading her toward the cabin door.

A rusty hinge announced them as they stepped inside. The cabin had only one room and was so much like the one that Cowslip had come from that she would not have been surprised to see Mariah and all the young'uns standing there. Even the few broken and dented pots that hung in the fireplace looked the same.

There was no real furniture. A few wooden boxes had been made into the shape of chairs and a larger one served as a table. Scattered about on the dirt floor were piles of blankets, and clothing hung from pegs driven into the walls. A few shuck ticks — bags full of corn-husks that were used for mattresses — had been tossed into one corner.

Five or six women were standing together in the center of the room, and they looked up quickly. Their faces were tense, as if they had expected someone else.

Something was wrong. For a moment Cowslip could not be sure what it was. Why was everyone so uneasy? Why was everyone so quiet?

That was it. The quietness. She had never seen slaves so quiet inside their own cabin. Usually they seemed to wake up from a walking sleep once they were away from the prying eyes and ears of the overseer, but they did not act that way tonight.

"Make yourself to home," Mehitabel urged. "You can meet the others directly."

Mehitabel left Cowslip standing beside the door and began talking to the women in low tones. They paid no attention to Cowslip now. Instead, they started chattering nervously among themselves, bobbing and clucking like hens. Cowslip noticed that their gaze often shifted to a young girl who looked to be about fifteen or sixteen. She sat on the floor with her back pressed rigidly against the cabin wall.

The girl looked different from any slave Cowslip had ever seen. Her dark-green waist and skirt were common enough, except for a white handkerchief, edged in lace, that was tucked into the band of her skirt. But instead of being a rich, glossy black, her skin was as soft a brown as autumn oak leaves. Now and then a tear left the girl's red-rimmed eyes and rolled down beside her slender nose.

Every few minutes one or another of the women went to her, patted her hand or stroked her shoulder, and said softly, "Don't you worry none, Reba. Everything will be all right."

What in tarnation was going on? Nothing made any sense to Cowslip. Was Reba sick or in some kind of trouble? Maybe she should try to help.

"Mercy me, Cowslip. You going to stand in that spot till you put down roots and grow?" Mehitabel shouted from across the room. She moved two chairs close to the big table and motioned for Cowslip to join her.

"I fetched down all that there was left from supper for you," Mehitabel said apologetically. She opened a large dinner napkin and took out a heel of bread and a small bowl of gravy. "Starting tomorrow, you'll likely eat your supper in the kitchen with the rest of us."

Cowslip nodded gratefully. It seemed more like days than hours since she had had breakfast in the slave pen. There had been no time to think about hunger during the long day, and now, with food in front of her, there was no time for words.

When she had finished the last of the bread and gravy, she leaned close to Mehitabel and whispered, "What's the matter with everybody?"

"They got a powerful lot on their minds tonight," Mehitabel said with a worried frown. "But it ain't got nothing to do with you, and I reckon it's high time they made you feel to home."

Taking Cowslip by the arm, Mehitabel led

her to a corner where all but the light-skinned girl were deep in conversation. They seemed to put away their worries for the moment and greeted Cowslip warmly as Mehitabel explained who they were: Sarah, the chambermaid; Chloella, the downstairs maid, who was stiffly starched and fine looking in a black uniform and white apron and dust cap; and Hag, the ancient, toothless laundress, who was so wrinkled that she looked as if she had spent the day inside her tubs of soapy water.

Cowslip was glad to be made welcome, but more than anything she wanted to meet Reba. She had to be in the middle of the mysterious things that were going on.

Finally Mehitabel led Cowslip across the room toward Reba, who, Mehitabel said, helped her in the kitchen. Before they got halfway to her, Reba jumped to her feet. "Listen," she shouted excitedly. "It's time!"

Cowslip strained her ears. At first she heard nothing, but finally she could make out the voice of a man singing in the night. Nobody moved as the deep rich voice grew stronger and stronger the nearer it came.

"Get on board, little children,
Get on board, little children,
Get on board, little children,
There's room for many a more."

"I know that song," Cowslip thought. She had heard it lots of times. Only it had always been a joyful, foot-stomping kind of song. It sure sounded different tonight.

"The gospel train's a-coming, I hear it just at hand, I hear the car wheels rumbling and rolling through the land.
I hear the train a-coming, she's coming round the curve. She's loosened all her steam and brakes and straining every nerve.
The fare is cheap and all can go, the rich and poor were there,
No second class aboard this train, no difference in the fare."

The women sat like stakes driven into the cabin floor, but their eyes were alive with brightness. Only Cowslip stirred restlessly. Was the song some kind of signal?

Of course it was. Why hadn't she thought of it before? Black folks' singing was practically a language by itself. It had to be, because the overseer was always straining his ears when slaves talked plain words. But they could talk about all kinds of things by singing the right songs, and laugh all the time at the overseer because he never did catch on. What was being talked about tonight? She listened to the words again.

"Get on board, little children,
Get on board, little children,
Get on board, little children,
There's room for many a more."

The singing grew fainter now, and fainter,
until it could not be heard anymore, and then
Reba burst into tears.

CHAPTER 5

Mehitabel lifted the sobbing girl into her arms. "Reba, honey," she said. "You just cry all you want to. It'll make you feel a whole lot better."

Reba clung to Mehitabel as the old cook sat down on a makeshift chair and gently rocked back and forth as if she were soothing a child.

Finally Mehitabel looked up at Cowslip and said quietly, "Tonight three field hands run off to freedom. That song you just heard was their signal to go. One of them is Reba's man, Percy. He's going up north to Canada to make a place for them and then he'll come back for her."

The other women were all looking at Cowslip

now, and she looked back at them, searching their faces, wondering how they could let themselves be in on such a foolish thing.

She wanted to shout at them, "What's the matter with you? Don't you know blacks can't never be free?" But something held her back.

Mehitabel's eyes were closed, and she crooned softly as the girl in her arms grew quiet.

"You feeling better now, Reba, honey?" she asked at last.

Reba nodded and sat up, but still she looked at the floor. "How long you think it will take them to get to the river?" she asked.

"Hard to say," Mehitabel said evasively.

Hag shook her head and let out a long, wheezy laugh. There's night patrols with dogs thick as gnats out there."

"Hag! You shush up that kind of talk," the cook scolded. "I reckon we'll know before morning. We'd best tend to the evening chores now. Just make the time go slower if we sit and wait."

Slowly the women began to stir, tidying up the cabin, mending clothes. Only Reba did not move. She sat stiffly against the cabin wall with her eyes closed tightly, but Cowslip knew that she was not asleep.

She's plain scared, that's all, Cowslip

thought. She scooted across the dirt floor and sat beside Reba.

The girl opened her eyes and looked at Cowslip in surprise. Then she nodded softly as if she understood. They sat side by side in silence for a long time, but finally Cowslip asked, "How come your Percy run away?"

Reba sighed and stared in the direction of the hot coals that lay on the hearth in a bright cluster, redder than the sunset. "For a long time now we've been looking to go up north to Canada, where colored can marry legal without the dread of our young'uns being sold away from us. Then Master said he was going to sell my Percy just as far south as wind would carry."

Reba paused, and a faint smile passed across her face, lighting her eyes almost to a twinkle.

"He was always saying that," she went on, "because Percy was such a rascal and was always causing Master all the trouble he could. But lately Master been saying that when he come back from market with a gang of new field hands, Percy's as good as sold. Today Master come back from market with them new slaves, so Percy had to run off. And he had to do it tonight."

Cowslip could not think of anything to say. The whole thing seemed hopeless any way she looked at it, but she could not say that to Reba.

The cabin was silent. The chores were all finished, but no one made a move to go to bed. Cowslip could feel the same uneasiness that had been in the air when she first entered the cabin. The feeling floated in like a fog and settled among the watchful women.

Cowslip felt uneasy too. Were there really night patrols with dogs, as Hag had said? What would happen to the men if they were caught? Would Reba get in trouble too? How could running away be worth the chances they were taking?

Reba pressed her ear against a splintered board. Suddenly she jumped up and cried in a high-pitched voice, "Something's gone wrong! I know it!"

Mehitabel lumbered to her feet and rushed over to the excited girl. "Sh. Now how we going to hear the signal with you making all that racket?"

Reba sank to the floor again and leaned wearily against the wall.

Hag shook her head. "Don't look good," she mumbled. "Been an awful long time. Don't look good at all."

Cowslip stood up and paced restlessly around the cabin. She could not bear to sit still any longer. She opened the door a crack and looked out. The darkened slave cabins stood out in the quiet night like rows of tombstones. Nothing moved.

Then, over by the corner of one of the farthest cabins, something caught her attention. Had that shadow stirred, or was she staring so hard that she was seeing things? Cowslip closed her eyes as if to clear them of sights that were not there, and then she opened them again, hurriedly looking toward the same spot.

This time she was sure the shadow had moved. It was a man walking, slowly weaving in and out among the cabins.

Might be Tanner, she thought, making his rounds.

Quickly she closed the door and went back to her place, keeping to herself what she had just seen. There was enough scaredness in the room already.

Then, all at once, everyone stopped fidgeting and started to listen. There was the faint sound of someone singing.

"No more auction block for me,
No more, no more,
No more auction block for me,
Many thousand gone."

The melody came in like a wisp of smoke, twirling through the cracked boards of the wall. It was the signal. The three men had made it to the river.

> "No more peck of corn for me,
> No more, no more,
> No more peck of corn for me,
> Many thousand gone.

> "No more pint of salt for me,
> No more, no more,
> No more pint of salt for me,
> Many thousand gone."

From around the room the women rushed toward Reba, some laughing, some crying. Even Hag had a wrinkled smile.

> "No more driver's lash for me,
> No more, no more,
> No more driver's lash for me,
> Many thousand gone."

Reba stood in the center of the cabin with brimming eyes and a look that was near rapture on her face. "He's done it! He's broke the chains!" she cried. "My Lord, I'm shouting, singing glad."

"Somebody fetch the kettle," Mehitabel ordered.

Sarah and Chloella lifted a huge three-legged iron pot out of the fireplace and laid it on its side in the center of the room, with its feet pointing toward the door. Slowly Reba knelt in front of the mouth of the pot. Her trembling fingers clutched the lace-edged handkerchief as she began to sing.

"No more auction block for me,
No more, no more,
No more auction block for me,
Many thousand gone."

Her voice was high and clear, and as she sang, the words spun around inside the kettle, trapped there so that no one beyond the cabin could hear them.

The women watched quietly as the hours of fear and waiting melted into song. After a while, Mehitabel began singing along with Reba, clapping and swaying back and forth as the tempo quickened and sounds of joy filled the kettle. One by one, the others joined in, singing as if they too had been set free.

Over and over, they poured the words into the iron pot as streams of tears and perspiration rolled side by side down their faces.

Only Cowslip stood in silence, speechless at what she saw. A long time later, when pure exhaustion had stopped the singing and everyone else was asleep, Cowslip lay awake trying to figure it all out.

Is it true? she wondered. Glory be! Are they really free?

CHAPTER 6

Job had told Cowslip that he would go with her in the morning to meet Mistress for the first time, but when morning came, he was nowhere to be found. Cowslip asked Mehitabel where he was, but the old cook quickly shushed her and warned her with a frown not to breathe a word to anyone that Job was not around.

Cowslip wondered if he had run off with Percy the night before, but she was afraid to ask. Besides, Mehitabel wasted no time in pushing her out of the kitchen and directing her up the stairs to Mistress's bedroom just as she had done the day before.

Cowslip half expected to find Job on the

bottom step again, but he was not there, so she trudged slowly up the long staircase and along the deep-piled carpet in the hallway, stopping in front of Mistress's polished oak door. She smoothed her dress all the way down from her shoulders to her knees and straightened her yellow bandanna.

"I can't stand out here all day," she thought. "I got to knock sometime, but, glory be, right now I'm shaky as a wet hound dog."

She listened to the pounding of her heart, but strangely the thumping sound she heard grew louder and louder until she knew that it could not be her heart. Was it footsteps? Was someone coming up the stairs?

Jerking around, she saw Tanner's head rising above the railing. He panted as he neared the top, and his face was knotted into an expression of rage. At the same instant he saw her.

"Hey, you," he cried. "Get down to the kitchen."

What could he want with her? The scowl on his face sent shivers down Cowslip's back, and she wished mightily that she had had the courage to knock while she had the chance. If she had, she would be safe inside her Mistress's room right now.

Tanner crossed the hallway in three strides.

His fingers toyed with the butt of the whip stuck in his belt as if they itched to use it.

"I said, get down to the kitchen!" he growled.

Just as his hand closed roughly around Cowslip's arm, the door opened and Mrs. Sprague stepped into the hall. She was a slender, pleasant-looking woman, not much taller than Cowslip, and she wore a bright-blue dressing gown of shimmery satin. Her dark-red hair was caught in a single braid that fell like a rope across her shoulder.

"What is going on out here?" she demanded.

"Three slaves ran off last night," said Tanner, squeezing Cowslip's arm so hard that it ached. "But don't you worry, ma'am. We'll find out how they got away and where they went if we have to put the whip to every slave on this plantation."

With that, Tanner moved toward the stairway, dragging Cowslip behind him.

"Where do you think you're taking *my* servant?"

Mistress's eyes were blazing, and Cowslip thought she looked a whole lot taller now.

Tanner stopped and let go of Cowslip's arm.

"To the kitchen," he answered awkwardly. "To question her along with the other house slaves."

"Leave her alone," Mistress commanded. "You know she's just arrived. She doesn't know anything."

"Yes, ma'am," Tanner murmured.

Cowslip watched with relief as he turned and stomped off toward the stairs. Why had Mistress taken up for her? she wondered. No white person had ever done a thing like that before.

"You must be Cowslip," said Mrs. Sprague. "I'm glad you're finally here. Come into my bedroom."

Her voice had lost its anger, but still her speech sounded strange. Her words were clipped short instead of rolling out slow and easy.

They stepped into the bedroom which, to Cowslip's amazement, was a jumble of dresses and crinoline petticoats. Trunks and carpetbags sat everywhere, and a hoop dangled from the bedpost. A tall wardrobe stood in one corner of the room, its doors open wide. A hatbox teetered on the topmost shelf, and other hatboxes were piled knee deep on the floor in front of it.

I'll need your help if I'm to have everything ready to leave tomorrow," Mrs. Sprague said pleasantly. Her dressing gown rustled softly as she made a sweeping gesture around the room, stopping to face Cowslip. "My father is ill in Ohio, and I must go to him. But with war breaking out all over the country, I don't dare take the children. They will be your responsibility while I'm gone. You are to sleep in the nursery and to stay with them at all times."

Mistress was silent for a moment, looking Cowslip over closely.

"My goodness, you're young," she said at last. "Have you ever cared for children before?"

"I helped Mariah in the childhouse back on the old plantation," Cowslip offered hopefully.

"I see," Mistress answered slowly. "Well, the first thing we must do is get you cleaned up. Look at yourself in my mirror. You surely can't begin your duties in that state."

Cowslip turned to the gilt-edged mirror that hung above Mistress's vanity table and cautiously looked at herself. Her heart jumped at the sight of the beautiful yellow bandanna tied tightly around her hair, but her cheeks were hollow and her round black eyes seemed almost too large for such a small face. Her dress, a worn sack-shaped garment made of coarse brown tow linen, was stiff with dirt and still smelled of the floor of the slave pen where she had spent the night waiting to be sold. Her bruised and calloused feet were almost white with dust.

"I suppose not, ma'am," she answered shyly.

"I'll have Job see to it that you get cleaned up and are given some decent clothes to wear," said Mistress.

Cowslip stared at the bellpull as Mistress reached for it. She was sure Job would not answer, but to her surprise there was a soft knock at the door a few minutes later. Mistress called out to him to come in, and Job entered the room, looking just as calm and elegant as he had the day before.

"Please see to it that Cowslip is bathed and properly dressed. She will be staying in the nursery and tending the children while I'm away."

Job bowed low and held the door of the bedroom open for Cowslip.

"I'll be waiting here for you," Mistress called after her. "Don't dawdle. There's much to be done."

"Yes, ma'am," said Cowslip, and she scurried out of the room and down the hallway with Job.

"I'm sorry that I wasn't able to take you to Mrs. Sprague this morning as I promised," said Job. "I was urgently needed elsewhere."

Cowslip glanced at Job out of the corner of her eye. She was more sure than ever that he had had something to do with the escape, and tingles raced up her back at the thought of it.

When they reached the kitchen, she was glad to see that Tanner was gone. Mehitabel, Mary, and Chloella stood beside the fireplace deep in conversation. Their faces were drawn, and Cowslip suspected that the ordeal with Tanner had been far from pleasant.

They greeted her solemnly, but when Job announced that Mistress had ordered that Cowslip be cleaned up, Mehitabel began to smile.

"That's it," she said with a chuckle. "Reba can go with Cowslip to the washhouse."

The others nodded agreement, and Mehitabel turned to Cowslip and added, "She's hiding in the pantry. We're trying to keep her out of Tanner's way if we can."

Trying to keep her from getting whipped, Cowslip thought. How can freedom be worth all that?

Chloella opened the pantry door and Reba tiptoed out. She looked tired and scared, and Cowslip felt sorry for her.

When the women were sure that the way was clear, they hurried the two girls off toward the washhouse. Reba led, following the path down the hill behind the big house. They stayed in the shadows of the slave cabins as much as they could, being careful not to make a sound. The inhabitants of the cabin would be hard at work now, but Tanner might choose this time to poke around the empty quarters looking for clues to the escape.

At the bottom of the hill, beyond the slave cabins, was a patch of woods. Reba ducked quickly among the trees, with Cowslip following close behind her. Even though the way was longer by this route, the girls did not dare cross the open barn lot.

All at once, Reba leaned against a tree and closed her eyes. She was panting as if she had just run a foot race, and a single tear made a path down her dusty cheek.

"Percy is surely long gone by now," said Cowslip, trying to sound reassuring. "Why, I bet he's pretty nearly there by now."

Reba opened her eyes. "Do you suppose?" she whispered.

Cowslip gave Reba's hand a warm squeeze, and the two girls dashed hand in hand the short distance remaining to the washhouse.

Once they were safe inside, the girls began laughing with a mixture of joy and relief. Hag rushed toward them, dropping her scrub board into the soapy water.

"Sh," she said with a frown, blowing suds all over their faces. "Tanner just left here," she warned. "He's liable to hear you and come back."

They choked back their giggles, and Reba soberly tiptoed to the door, opened it a crack, and looked outside.

"There ain't no sign of him," she said. "But I'll keep watch."

Guessing why Cowslip had come, Hag lifted another washtub off a peg on the wall. There were tubs of all sizes hanging behind the enormous stove, where spewing kettles kept the wash water hot. Hag poured steaming water into the tub, refilled the kettles from a bucket of cold well water beside the stove, and motioned for Cowslip to get into her bath. Cowslip left her dress on the floor in a small heap, where it looked like an old potato sack, and climbed into the tub, taking the square of homemade yellow soap that Hag handed to her.

"You skin and bones, child." Hag clicked her tongue. "Mehitabel will have to fatten you up from the table leavings. Lucky for you the Colonel likes to eat hearty."

The warm water soothed Cowslip's tired body, and she lay back, resting her head on the rim of the tub. She closed her eyes, almost lulled to sleep by the warmth of the water. But soon the bath began to cool. Hag poured another kettle of warm water into the tub and pulled the yellow bandanna off Cowslip's head.

"How come you did that?" Cowslip demanded.

"You got to wash your head, don't you?" Hag answered curtly. Then, leaning close and inspecting Cowslip's hair she said, "Land sakes, you're lousy as a pet pig. Hold your breath."

With that she pushed on Cowslip's shoulders, ducking her under the water. Cowslip came up sputtering. She heard Hag cackle and the next instant felt dozens of tiny lice racing out of her hair and down her neck and face, trying to escape the deluge. Twice more Hag pushed her under the water until she was satisfied that all the lice were gone. Then she took the yellow bandanna and swished it around in the soapy water, hanging it on the handle of a warming kettle to dry.

When Cowslip had finished bathing, Hag opened a battered trunk and took out a pair of long white underdrawers and a matching camisole.

"Try these on for size," she said, handing them to Cowslip.

It took Cowslip a moment to figure out how to put them on, and then she could not help laughing at herself as she looked down at the strange-looking garb.

Hag looked her over and frowned. "They're a mite big," she said. "But you'll grow into them. Here's a petticoat. And try this. It ought to fit you good."

Cowslip gasped. Hag was holding out a dress. It was made of bright-blue calico with tiny red, yellow, and green flowers sprinkled all over it. The edges of the white collar and cuffs were worn, but the dress was clean and stiffly starched.

"That's for me?" Cowslip asked.

Hag nodded, opening the door of the stove and tossing Cowslip's old dress into the fire. "You know, girl, you're mighty lucky to get to work for Mistress. She comes from the North and don't cotton much to slaving, and she'll treat you right as any white folk I ever heard tell of."

Reba scowled. "Well, then," she snapped. "Why don't she turn us loose? White folks is all the same, far as I can see. I don't want nothing to do with none of them, and when my Percy comes for me, I won't never have to again."

"Running away is nothing but foolishness," Hag said. "How much you know about what you'll find up north, supposing you ever get there? You are what you are, and it's high time you learned to make the best of it."

Cowslip tied the damp yellow bandanna over her hair. She pulled on heavy stockings and pushed her feet into the coarse black shoes that Hag had set out for her. She wiggled her toes around inside the shoes, pretending not to hear what they were saying. Yesterday she had been sure of things, sure that Hag was right. But today everything was a puzzle. There had been something about the look on Reba's face when she was waiting for the signal last night and something about the joy of the women when the good news finally came that had set her to wondering.

"Someone's coming!" Reba whispered hoarsely.

"Quick. Over here," cried Hag. She pointed to a pile of dirty clothes on the floor. Reba crouched down beside it, and together Cowslip and Hag covered her with the clothes.

A moment later the door opened and Mehitabel rushed into the washhouse.

"I just had to find out if you got here all right," she said, breathless from her long walk from the big house.

Reba poked her head up through the dirty clothes. "You sure gave us a fright," she said with a smile. "We thought you was Tanner."

At that moment the door burst open and Tanner strode into the room.

"I thought it might be smart to follow you," he said to Mehitabel. Turning to Reba, he growled, "Come along. Colonel Sprague wants to talk to you."

CHAPTER 7

Slowly Reba rose out of the pile of dirty clothes. Cowslip watched in amazement as she squared her shoulders, raised her chin, and pranced right past Tanner toward the door just as though she were somebody special.

"Sure is a mighty peculiar way for a person to act who's about to get in trouble," Cowslip mused.

Across the room, fat tears rolled down Mehitabel's face as she watched Tanner lead Reba out of the washhouse. "Mercy me," she sobbed. "Oh, mercy. Look what I done."

Cowslip went to the old cook and patted her arm.

Mehitabel sighed. "We'd best be getting back to the big house before we get in trouble our own selves," she said in a whispery voice.

They walked back in silence. Cowslip tried not to think about what was most likely happening to Reba at that very moment. All the same, she could not get the spunky girl out of her mind. She liked Reba, even though she did have saucy ways sometimes. *She* wouldn't have hung around any old slave market digging her toe into the dirt and telling Bible stories to herself. She would have run away, and she would have laughed over her shoulder at her master as she went too. Still, there was a soft way about Reba as well. It showed when she talked about Percy.

Cowslip clenched her fists as she entered the big house, and wished with all her might that Colonel Sprague would be easy on Reba. Then she hurried up the stairs to Mistress's room and knocked softly on the door.

A smile spread quickly over Mrs. Sprague's face when she opened the door and saw Cowslip standing there. "Goodness. You look so much better," she said pleasantly. "I'm glad that Hag was able to find some clothes to fit you."

Cowslip had completely forgotten about her new clothes, and her pulse quickened at Mistress's approval. Gingerly she approached the mirror, but before she could catch a glimpse of herself, Mistress called to her.

"We have lots to do today, Cowslip, so let me show you the nursery first."

Mistress bustled down the hall, and Cowslip tagged along behind her. They stopped at a closed door, and Mistress held up her hand.

"Shhh," she cautioned. "Our baby, Toby, is asleep in here. The other children — Joel, who is four, and Laura Margaret, who is seven — have gone into town with their father to arrange my transportation to Ohio."

They tiptoed into the spacious corner room. It was light and airy, with windows on two sides. A pair of small beds, and a cradle, where Toby napped peacefully, lined one end of the room. Dolls and other toys filled the other end.

"Job will set up a bed for you in this corner," Mistress whispered, gesturing toward a spot by a window, where the branches of a tall oak tree brushed lazily across the glass. "Tonight you're to sleep in the white cabin, but while I'm away you're to stay with the children night and day."

Mrs. Sprague's face then clouded into a frown.

"There will be absolutely no excuse for you to leave the children. You will be responsible for their health and safety at all times. I'm not happy about leaving them in your care to begin with. You're young. You're inexperienced. However, the war makes traveling too dangerous for me to take them with me."

Cowslip swallowed hard. "Yes, ma'am," she said. Caring for the Sprague children would be a bigger job than she had expected, and she hoped that Mistress would not be gone very long.

Mrs. Sprague had spoken about the war again, just as she had done earlier in the day. Cowslip remembered hearing some talk about a war and about a white man named Mr. Lincoln who wanted to set the slaves free, but she hadn't believed that it was true. No white man would ever do a thing like that.

"Come along now," Mistress said. "I'll explain your duties in detail while we're getting my things packed."

Together they filled what seemed like an endless number of trunks and carpetbags with Mrs. Sprague's clothes while Cowslip concentrated hard on every word that Mistress said. There was so much to remember. How would she ever learn it all? She was to feed Laura Margaret and Joel their midday meal in the kitchen, but they were to have breakfast and supper in the dining room with Master. Bedtime was right after supper. She could swat them if they were a little bit naughty, but Master would handle anything more serious. And Toby, who was only eight months old, would need to be either changed or fed every time she turned around. The list of instructions went on and on. How could she possibly keep them all straight?

Late that afternoon, when the last petticoat had been tucked inside a bag and the last pair of shoes stuffed inside a trunk, Mistress picked up Toby, who had been happily crawling among the bags and trunks since awakening from his nap, and sank onto the giant feather bed with a sigh.

"Well, Cowslip, we've certainly put in a day," she said, gently bouncing Toby on her lap.

"Yes, ma'am," Cowslip answered awkwardly, wondering what she should be doing now.

"You may go now," said Mistress, as if she had been reading Cowslip's mind. "I won't be needing you anymore today."

"Yes, ma'am."

Cowslip backed timidly out of the room and hurried through the house and out into the sunshine, relieved to be away from Mistress's sight. Mrs. Sprague was a kind and gentle woman, but still, she was the mistress, and she was expecting an awful lot from Cowslip in the days to come.

Suppertime was a while off yet, so Cowslip ambled toward the white cabin, reciting to herself the long list of chores that Mistress had given her. When she reached the cabin door, she heard faint sounds coming from inside. She stopped and listened for a moment. Someone was crying.

Reba! she thought with a start. She banged the door open and rushed inside. Reba lay sprawled across the dirt floor, the back of her dress torn open. Across her back were the stripes of five raw and bleeding lash marks.

Lightning-hot anger flashed through Cowslip. She slammed the door and raced to Reba. "Glory be! Look what they done to you."

Reba raised her head and looked at Cowslip with blazing eyes. "I didn't tell them *nothing*!"

"Don't talk about it now," Cowslip said. She dragged a shuck tick out of the corner, fluffed and patted it to make it as comfortable as possible, and gently helped Reba to her feet.

"Here. I fixed a bed for you. You'll rest a mite easier."

Reba sank onto the pallet panting. She lay on her stomach with her eyes closed, her whole body shaking with sobs.

Cowslip stared down at the angry welts on the girl's back. "Glory be. Glory be," she murmured over and over in disbelief. Her stomach was doing flip-flops and her knees were as weak as water. It wasn't right to whip a person, especially a person as little and weak as Reba was, for all her saucy talk. She reached out a hand and patted Reba softly on the shoulder.

"But then," she told herself sternly, "it's just as wrong to stand here gawking instead of doing something to ease her pain."

Cowslip raced to the single pump that supplied water for all the slaves. She filled the bucket and hurried back to the cabin, searching in vain for a piece of soft clean cloth to use to bathe Reba's wounds. Then she thought of her own petticoat. Slowly she raised her skirt and looked down at it. It was as soft and white as a cloud and the only petticoat she had ever worn. If only she could find something else.

Reba moaned softly from the pallet, and Cowslip looked again at her raw back. With a jerk, she ripped the petticoat off and dropped it into the bucket of water. She wrung out the cloth and tore it into two pieces, one large and one small. Gently she patted the wounds with the larger piece until she was satisfied that they were clean. Then she rinsed the cloth and spread it across Reba's torn back.

"This here cool water ought to take the burn

out some," Cowslip whispered. Fishing around in the bucket until she found the smaller piece of cloth, Cowslip mopped the dirt and perspiration from Reba's face.

Reba did not stir. Every now and then her eyelids fluttered and she looked up at Cowslip with pain-filled eyes, but each time she dropped back into a feverish sleep.

Cowslip sat on the floor beside Reba for a long time, bathing her back over and over again with the cool water. Cowslip was sure that it was getting close to suppertime. Her empty stomach told her so, and so did the dusky grayness that was slowly filling the cabin. Perhaps she should go up to the kitchen and bring back some food for Reba and herself.

Just then Reba opened her eyes. She raised her head and looked first at Cowslip and then around at the darkening room.

"You been sitting with me all this time?" she asked, as if it were more than she could believe.

Cowslip nodded. "How you feeling?"

"My back don't hurt near so bad. Guess it's turned sort of numb. My jaws sure do ache, though, from gritting my teeth."

"You hungry? I was fixing to go up to the kitchen and get us some supper."

"I guess I got to keep my strength up, hungry or not," said Reba, propping herself up on one elbow. "But how come you're doing all this for me?"

"I don't know," said Cowslip shyly. "I feel real sorry about your back, and I guess I admire how you're always prancing around and sticking out your chin like you're something pretty special. Takes a heap of bravery for a slave to do something like that."

A strange look crossed Reba's face. "You really think I'm brave?" she asked quietly.

"I sure do. Besides, you're fixing to run away, ain't you? I had a chance to run away at the slave market yesterday, but I was too plain scared. I just stood there talking myself out of it until I lost my chance."

Reba stared at Cowslip. She looked as if she were going to cry. "You want to know something that I ain't never told nobody?"

Cowslip swallowed hard and nodded.

Reba hesitated a moment and then looked deep into Cowslip's eyes as she spoke. "I been scared every minute since I been born."

Cowslip shook her head in disbelief. "You scared?" she said. "Then how come you're going to run off?"

"Sometimes being scared's what makes you run. I run off once when I was nine or ten, but it wasn't bravery made me do it. A spiteful old slave named Zula told me that the reason I was such a light-brown color was because my pappy was a white man. She said he was the driver on this here plantation and that when Colonel Sprague found out that he had forced hisself on my ma, he run him off, and that's when he hired Tanner. Anyway, when I heard that, I hated myself. Partly it was because I was born black and a slave, but I hated myself worse because part of me was white. And I was scared of what might happen to me for being all mixed up like that, so I run off.

"I wanted to get lost or maybe get swallowed up by a bear, but I couldn't find much food and after a while I wanted to go home something miserable. About four days later some of Master's searchers found me sleeping under a tree. When I got home, my ma whipped me within an inch of salvation. Then she set me down and told me that it was sinful to hate myself and that I was always to remember that I was a human person same as all white folks, same as all blacks, and that God, His own self, makes every single human person in the world.

"She said there was a word for knowing deep down that you're a human person. The word is 'dignity.' And clear up till the day she died she kept telling me that I was duty bound to have dignity every minute I was alive. She said dignity would help me not to be afraid. But it's mighty hard to get the hang of having dignity. I expect I never did, because most times when I act brave, I'm just covering up for being scared."

Cowslip shook her head as if to protest, but the lump that filled her throat kept her from speaking. After a moment she got to her feet. "Guess I better fetch us some supper now," she managed to whisper.

She walked to the cabin door. Then she stopped and spun around.

"I *still* think you're brave," she sputtered. "Glory be, I think you're the bravest person I ever saw!"

Then, turning, she ran out of the cabin and up the hill.

CHAPTER 8

For the next few days the plantation was in an uproar. The Colonel questioned everyone, even Cowslip and the other new slaves who had been bought the same day the three field hands had escaped. When that did not work, there were whippings for several more slaves who were known to have been close friends of the runaways. Still, no one talked.

Search parties were organized. Men on horseback thundered on and off the plantation night and day, but it was all for nothing.

No trace could be found of Percy and his companions.

As often as she could, Cowslip sneaked down to the white cabin to see Reba, but most of the time she had all that she could handle minding the children. Baby Toby was a smile wrapped in diapers whenever he caught sight of her. Mehitabel said that she had never seen anybody pacify Toby the way Cowslip did.

Laura Margaret was a quiet ladylike child. She spent long afternoons drinking tea with her dolls.

The thing that kept Cowslip busiest was chasing Joel. It seemed to her that he covered more of the plantation in a day than all of the field hands put together. She couldn't even keep him in the house. As soon as Cowslip turned her head, he was hightailing it for the river, or he was in the fields pulling big green worms off the tobacco leaves to feed to his baby brother. He tried to climb into the well and into the pen with the brood sow, and he usually did it just as she was getting Toby to sleep or when Laura Margaret most urgently needed sympathy for a sick doll or a broken teacup. Then, with Toby astraddle her hip, Cowslip would run after Joel, dragging Laura Margaret behind her.

Most of the time she did not mind Joel's

tricks. It gave her a free kind of feeling to run through the grass and kick the dirt clods in the fields. Sometimes she laughed out loud just to think of herself, a slave, paddling a white child for running off.

But now and then Joel carried things too far. One hot afternoon when the sun was beating down unmercifully Cowslip settled the children beneath a shade tree where the back lawn dipped away from the house and the sparkling river winked at them from behind low-mounded hills. A soft breeze was blowing, and Toby cooed contentedly on a pallet in the grass. Laura Margaret worked on her lessons, laboriously printing letters into her copybook while Cowslip brushed her silky blond hair. Joel paraded around the yard like a soldier, stomping on freshly built anthills and scattering their inhabitants with a stick.

Cowslip was paying little attention to Joel and did not notice when he grew tired of his game and tiptoed up behind her. With a snatch, he grabbed the yellow bandanna off her head and streaked down the hill toward the river.

"My bandanna!" Cowslip shrieked. "You bring that back here this minute!"

Joel kept right on going at breakneck speed. Cowslip was furious. She plopped Toby onto her hip so hard that he began to howl. She jerked Laura Margaret into a run, sending the copybook tumbling through the grass.

All Cowslip could think about was her precious bandanna, and visions of it floating away forever in the river's current set her legs churning over the ground after Joel.

She might have caught him if Laura Margaret had not stumbled. By the time Laura Margaret had recovered her balance, Joel was out of sight in the band of scrubby trees that fringed the riverbank.

"I'll never find him now," Cowslip thought miserably. "There are just too many places to hide."

Just then Joel darted in front of her, waving the bandanna like a bright flag, and she was after him again, ducking under low-hanging branches and sidestepping around thorny bushes.

By now Laura Margaret was crying too, so when Cowslip saw Joel scurry between a patch of bramble and a clump of rocks that looked like a drop-off into the river, she sat her under the nearest tree and stuck Toby into her lap.

"I'll be back directly," she told Laura Margaret hoarsely, breathless from the run.

The rocks scraped her on one side and the bramble scratched on the other, but she squeezed in after him, fearful now that he might fall into the swirling river.

"Joel! Where are you?" she called. He was nowhere in sight.

Then she saw the yellow bandanna waving from a crevice in the rocks. It disappeared again, and when she reached the spot, she found an opening large enough to crawl into that was completely hidden from view by the undergrowth.

He must be in there, she thought, plunging into the darkness.

Once through the opening, she could stand up. As her eyes adjusted to the dim light, she realized for the first time where she was. She was in a cave, and Joel was probably hiding in another room. She hoped so, anyway.

"I'm fixing to come looking for you, Joel Sprague," she yelled. She made the words sound as threatening as she could. "You might just as well come out now."

Her voice sounded strange to her as it echoed among the damp rocks, but there was no reply.

The air in the cave was heavy, but it seemed refreshingly cool after chasing Joel through the hot sunshine. She could hear the sound of water gently plopping against the rocks and she headed toward it. Rounding a corner, she found herself in a larger room of the cave. The sound of the river was louder, and at one end of the room she could see daylight streaking in through a narrow slit.

Water was dripping everywhere, making the floor of the cave slippery to walk on, so she made her way toward the light carefully, concentrating on every step.

The narrow opening looked as if it had once been the riverside entrance to the cave. Now a huge rock blocked it so that there was not enough room even for a child to slip through.

That's a relief, she thought. At least he didn't jump into the river.

She turned around and peered into the dim room, trying to see the figure of a small boy among the juts and crevices that shaped the walls. Finally she did see him. He was crouched against the far wall, grinning at her and holding his hands behind his back.

"Thank the Lord, you're safe," Cowslip murmured. She hurried toward him, screwing up her face into a scowl and demanding, "Where's my bandanna?"

Joel laughed and jumped up as if to run, but she caught him, scooping him into her arms. As she lifted him, she felt something dangling near her feet. It was a blanket, the coarse kind used by the slaves. Joel had been sitting on it.

Slowly she put Joel down and looked around her.

On the floor nearby were crumbs of ash cake and stone jars filled with water.

"What have we found?" she said, and a terrible dread settled over her.

"I got a feeling deep in my bones that we better be hightailing it out of here," Cowslip whispered. She steered Joel in the direction of the opening of the cave.

Then, suddenly, she heard men's voices, and she realized they, too, were inside the cave. Someone must have come in the same way she and Joel had come, and they were standing in the small room talking.

"I didn't touch anything," one of the men was saying. "I left it just the way I found it for you to see."

Another man grunted in approval. Cowslip could hear footsteps coming closer, and she clutched Joel tightly and stared at the opening between the two rooms of the cave, wishing with all her might that she knew a magic spell that would make her invisible.

"In here," the first man said.

Cowslip closed her eyes and held her breath.

CHAPTER 9

All at once, Joel wrenched himself from her hold and shouted, "Papa!"

Cowslip opened her eyes. She was face to face with Colonel Sprague. A man she had never seen before stood beside him.

There was silence for a moment, and then the hollow cave rang with the sound of her name.

"Cowslip!"

"Yes, sir, Colonel Sprague," she blurted out. "You see, Joel here likes to run off and he snatched my bandanna and took off at a run and I chased him clean down to this here cave, and we was just fixing to head back to the big house and that's the truth."

Colonel Sprague spat a wad of tobacco onto the slimy cave floor and regarded her sternly. He looked down at Joel, who was fidgeting on one foot and fiddling with the yellow bandanna.

Cowslip lowered her eyes, hoping that her master would not see how frightened she was. Her heart thumped furiously — so loud, in fact, that she was sure he could hear it.

"Get out of here and don't come back!" he ordered. Squinting his eyes and putting his face close to hers, he added, "If you ever breathe a word about this place and what you've seen here, I'll have your hide good and proper."

Cowslip could not help trembling as she reached out for Joel's hand. "The only reason I'm not getting whipped is because he's too busy seeing about this cave," she thought.

She ignored the sting of the brambles as she almost dragged Joel out of the cave into the sunlight, which splattered through the branches of the trees and landed on the ground in blobs and puddles like spilled water.

She grabbed the bandanna from Joel and tied it around her head without breaking her stride. "Hurry up, child," she urged when he bent down to examine a rock.

"Cowslip. Is that you?"

Laura Margaret's head bobbed up from behind a boulder.

"Glory be! I plumb forgot. Are you all right? Where's Toby?"

"I hid him back here when I heard horses coming," said Laura Margaret. She pointed proudly to a spot behind the rock. "I was too scared even to look until I heard you. I sure am glad you're here."

Toby was asleep on the grass, but at the sound of Cowslip's voice he opened his eyes and smiled broadly.

As Cowslip stooped to pick him up, she heard voices coming from the direction of the cave. Her arms swooped down like the wings of a bird, pressing Joel and Laura Margaret to the ground.

"Sh," she cautioned Laura Margaret. "It's your pappy, but he's powerful angered. We got to stay out of his way."

Laura Margaret nodded and stroked Toby's forehead to keep him from fussing.

Colonel Sprague and the other man were in a small clearing nearby, and Cowslip could hear what they were saying.

"Looks like they used this cave for a hideaway," said the stranger. "They could have stayed there three or four days and then left by boat, probably some time at night."

"They had to have help," the Colonel said slowly. "A hidden cave that looks out onto the river, blankets, food, water, and a boat that carries them off in the middle of the night — a bunch of field hands couldn't have managed all that by themselves."

"You think it was the Underground Railroad?" the other man asked.

"Probably," answered Colonel Sprague. "But when I catch those runaways, I'll make such examples out of them that no slave of mine will ever think of running away again."

Cowslip shuddered as she listened to the men talk. The Underground Railroad always conjured up pictures in her mind of a long tunnel dug below the earth and a slave jumping in at one end.

There had been whispers among the slaves on the other plantation that the Underground Railroad was not a train or a tunnel or anything like that, but was really people who passed slaves along to freedom like water buckets to a fire. That did not seem any more likely to her than the hole in the ground, but she did not have time to think about it now.

The two men mounted their horses and rode

away, and Cowslip picked up Toby and wearily led the children back across the sloping meadow toward the big house. She had been too far away to see the look in Colonel Sprague's eyes when he threatened vengeance against the runaway slaves, but she had known by the sound of his voice that he meant it.

"I got to stop him," she thought. "I got to get revenge on him for what he did to Reba too, and I know a surefire way to do it."

The children were tired from their adventure, and all three curled up for naps as soon as they got back to the house. Cowslip usually stayed in the room with them when they napped, mending and picking up toys. Today she tiptoed out as soon as she was sure they were sleeping and slipped down the stairs as silently as a shadow. No one was about, and she quickly made her way to the kitchen.

She opened the door a crack and peered in. Only Mehitabel was there, kneading dough and humming to herself.

The door squeaked as Cowslip closed it behind her and Mehitabel jumped, sending little clouds of flour into the air.

"Mercy me, girl. You gave me a fright," she said. She tried to frown, but a big grin spread over her face instead.

"I got to have help," Cowslip began. She

knew that she could not stay in the kitchen long. "I got something powerful important that's got to be wrote down."

This time Mehitabel succeeded in frowning. "Mercy me," she whispered. "Don't you know it's against the law for a slave to know how to write?"

"Course I know. But this is terrible important."

Mehitabel began kneading the dough again, shaking her head and muttering something that Cowslip could not hear. Finally she looked up. "If you're bound and determined," she said sternly, "go see Job. But mind you, it had better be as important as you say, and you'd better not let nobody catch you, neither."

Of all the slaves on the plantation, why did it have to be Job? Cowslip thought. She was uncomfortable around him. He always acted as though he knew something that nobody else knew and as if knowing it made him special. He seemed to look down at her from a mountaintop, and his voice was a quiet rumble, like faraway thunder on a hot summer night.

But there was no other way. She would have to go to Job for help if she was going to get revenge on Colonel Sprague, and she would do it tonight as soon as everyone was asleep.

Cowslip thought the day would never end. The sun seemed to be stuck in the afternoon sky, stubbornly refusing to be pulled from its lofty perch. Finally sunset came. It was Cowslip's favorite time of day, because Toby was always asleep then, and she would send Joel and Laura Margaret, all scrubbed and combed, down to the dining room to have supper with their father. Often, slipping quietly down the stairs so as not to disturb Master while he was eating, she left the house and sat alone on the back stoop, waiting for Mehitabel to bring what was left from the white folks' meal out to the summer kitchen for the house slaves to eat for supper. Cowslip loved to sit there, gazing off in the direction of the river, where the rosy glow of the setting sun greeted her like a warm smile mirroring her gladness that another day was almost over.

But today she hardly noticed the river or the sunset. She had plans to make, and she was so absorbed in thinking about them that she did not hear Hag running up the path from the slave cabins until she called out.

"Get Mehitabel. Tell her Reba's done got herself infected."

Cowslip burst into the kitchen and shouted the terrible news to Mehitabel without even looking to see if it was safe.

"Mercy me, mercy me," was all the old cook could say for a moment. Then, suddenly, she hurried from the room and returned a moment later with a handful of dried tobacco leaves.

Together Cowslip, Mehitabel, and Hag raced to the white cabin. They could hear Reba moaning as they opened the door.

Cowslip gasped at the first sight of her friend. Reba was lying on her stomach on a shuck tick, a blanket covering her legs. Across her back the lash marks were swollen and purple, and her face was drawn with pain. Chloella sat on the floor beside her, bathing her face with cool water.

Mehitabel set right to work crushing the tobacco leaves. Then she put them into a battered tin bowl and added water, stirring the mixture until it was almost a paste.

"This here poultice will draw out the infection," she said as she patted it over Reba's back. The girl winced, but she did not make a sound.

Cowslip watched helplessly. She ached for Reba and hated Colonel Sprague for having her whipped. But he would be sorry — she would see to that.

Time dragged by, and Reba's fever went higher and higher.

"You and me can't stay no longer," Mehitabel told Cowslip at last. "You got to get the young'uns to bed, and I got to tend my kitchen. Colonel Sprague finds out we're down here instead of where we ought to be, we'll get the same as Reba."

Cowslip nodded and started slowly for the big house. She knew that Mehitabel was right, and she knew that Hag and Chloella would do all that could be done for Reba, but she longed to stay with her friend.

Luckily, they had not been missed. Cowslip dressed the children for bed, heard their prayers, and impatiently waited for the house to grow quiet for the night.

She listened for a long time. Everyone seemed to be asleep, but how could she be sure that Colonel Sprague was not working late at his big desk in the library? It would be terrible if she crept down the stairs only to meet Master coming up to bed.

That left only one thing for her to do. It was a hot summer night, and the nursery windows were open wide. She slid over the sill, moving quickly before she lost her nerve, and clamped her hands firmly around a branch of the oak tree that grew beside the house. She inched her foot out until it rested on a branch, and swung away from the window and into the tree, stopping when she bumped against the trunk. It was a sturdy tree, with branches well placed for climbing, and in a moment she had landed safely on the ground.

She stopped to get her breath. All of the lights in the big house were out but one. In Job's room on the ground floor a candle sat inside the window, and its wavering flame cast shadows that looked like dancing ghosts on the ground below.

Cowslip could see Job sitting in a chair staring at the wall in front of him as if he were in some sort of trance. Why did he always act so strange? She almost wished that she had never come.

"I got to put my scaredness under my feet and stand on it," she thought. Then she slowly raised her hand and tapped on the windowpane.

CHAPTER 10

At first Job did not seem to hear her. He kept right on staring at the wall, as if she were just a tree branch scratching against the window in the breeze.

She tapped harder, this time with her knuckles, and he looked up. Rising, he crossed the room toward the window, and Cowslip pressed her face close so that the frail light from the candle would show him who she was.

He did not look so frightening now as he smiled down at her. He was not wearing his dark red coat, and his fancy shirt was open at the neck. .

He raised the window and said in his quiet way, "Cowslip? What is it, girl?"

She could not get the words out fast enough. "I've got something powerful important that's got to be wrote down," she sputtered.

"Sh. You're going to wake Master," Job whispered. "Give me your hand."

He pulled her into the room and signaled for her to be quiet while he listened at the door. Cowslip stood awkwardly in the center of the room and waited.

She gazed around her. Job's quarters did not look as if they could possibly be a part of the rest of the house. Instead of fancy wallpaper and heavy draperies, the walls were a bleak white, and there was a small iron bed, similar to her own, in one corner, with a coarse gray blanket folded neatly at the foot. The only other piece of furniture was the straight wooden chair on which Job had been sitting. The beautiful red butler's coat hung on the back of it, looking elegantly out of place.

"It's all right," Job said at last. He motioned for her to sit down on the chair and seated himself on the edge of the bed. "Now tell me again what it is that I can do for you."

Cowslip took a deep breath and swallowed

hard. This was her only chance, and she had to say it just right.

"I'd be forever grateful to you if you'd write down Colonel Sprague's name on a piece of paper. I aim to put a curse on him for being so mean to slaves."

"A curse?"

"Yes, sir," Cowslip answered proudly. "You see, back on the old plantation I learned about spells and curses from an old hoodoo woman named Mariah. She said to write down the name of your enemy on a piece of paper and to put the paper in a dead bird's mouth. When that dead bird dries up, troubles and misfortunes will shower down on your enemy like leaves in an autumn windstorm. Them's Mariah's very words. I know the curse works. I seen it with my own eyes."

Cowslip wished secretly that she could be as sure of the powers of the curse as she sounded. After all, it was because of this curse that she had been sold, but she would have to take her chances on its turning out right this time, because it was the only curse she knew.

"I see," Job replied matter-of-factly. "But why don't you write it yourself?"

"Glory be. I can't write," Cowslip gasped.

"Then it's time you learned."

Job pulled the bed out a little way and drew a small slate and a piece of chalk from a hiding place.

Cowslip watched in amazement. She started to speak, but Job held up his hand for silence.

"You are about to tell me that writing is against the law for blacks."

Cowslip nodded, thinking that he must have the power to read minds too.

"But do you know *why* it's against the law?"

"Yes, sir," she murmured. "I expect it's the will of the Lord."

Job slapped his hands against his thighs in disgust. "The will of the Lord," he echoed. "What makes you believe that it's the will of the Lord?"

"Why, the preacher that used to come to the old plantation read it right out of the Bible lots of times," Cowslip said.

"Did you read it yourself? Or did you let Master's preacher tell you what it said?"

Cowslip did not answer. In one way she understood what Job was trying to say, but in another way it did not make any sense.

"Cowslip," Job said gently, "I'm going to try to explain to you why it's against the law for you to read or write and, perhaps most important of all, why you've been told that slavery is the will of the Lord."

Cowslip looked anxiously toward the window. This was not what she had come for. Half of her wanted to hear what he was going to say, but the other half wanted to run.

"Chains and whips can only enslave your body," Job began, "not your mind. And if your mind is free, you're going to want your body to be free too. Master can't take a chance on that happening, because then you wouldn't work so hard, and you'd cause him all kinds of trouble. If you could read, you'd find out what life is like far away from here, where it's held to be a sin for one man to own another, and you'd run away."

While he talked, Job picked up the slate and laid it in his lap. Cowslip watched as his strong, steady hand began to write a word. It was not just a bunch of swirls like she made when she drew in the dust with a stick. His fingers knew where each line should go before he ever made it.

"Master takes every precaution to keep his slaves as mindless as a flock of chickens. To him they're animals, and they come to think of themselves as animals too. Master never lets slaves think of themselves as human beings or allows them to have a will of their own, because when he tosses them a few specks of food and a rag or two to keep themselves warm, he wants them to be grateful.

Then he brings a man to the plantation that he calls a preacher to tell the blacks that slavery is the will of the Lord."

Emotion throbbed in Job's low voice, and his eyes were ablaze as he spoke.

"But you, Cowslip, can rise above all this. You can start right now to set yourself free."

These last words were as startling as a slap, and Cowslip stared first at Job and then at the slate. She wanted desperately to believe him — he made it all seem possible. But still, it sounded too good to be true. Maybe his mind was free, like he said, and maybe that was what made him so different from the other slaves, almost peaceful with his quiet eyes and soft voice. Still, she needed more proof.

"Can you read, Job?" she asked.

"Oh, yes. I can read."

"Well, if you can read," she challenged, "read to me from the Bible. Read me the part that the preacher read where it says that blacks always got to be slaves. Then I'll know for sure if it's the will of the Lord."

Job was thoughtful for a moment.

"No," he said slowly. "I won't read the Bible to you, but I'll do something better. I'll teach you to read, so you can find out what it says for yourself."

Now it was Cowslip's turn to be thoughtful.

"I don't know," she whispered, still half afraid.

"It would be so easy," Job said. Excitement rose in his voice. "I would help you. Laura Margaret's first primer has been put away, but I know where it is. I could get it for you and, during the day, while the children nap, you could practice reading out of it. Then at night you could come here. No one would ever know."

Cowslip stood up and moved slowly toward the window. "I'll have to think about it," she said, shaking her head. "I'll let you know."

Job nodded solemnly.

"Wait just a moment," he said. "I almost forgot something."

He reached down to the hiding place behind the bed and brought out a scrap of paper, a quill, and a small pot of ink. He sat down on the bed and, using the slate as a table, wrote something on the paper.

Cowslip's heart beat fast. It was the same word that he had written on the slate while he was talking. She was going to get what she had come for, after all.

He handed the paper to her, and she took it eagerly. "Oh, thank you," she said. "Oh, thank you so much."

"Just one thing," he said, pointing a finger at her. "Don't use this in your spell."

"Why not?" Cowslip asked.

Taking the paper from her hand, he held it up so that she could see the word written on it.

"It says 'Cowslip,'" he told her.

Her knees turned soft as lard as she stared at the black marks on the paper. "My name?" she whispered. "My name can be wrote down?"

Job was smiling the kindest smile that she had ever seen, and he folded the paper and pressed it into her hand. "You go now," he said. "And you think about what I've said. Later we'll talk again."

Cowslip crawled out of the window and scrambled up the tree to the open nursery window, scarcely aware of what she was doing. Her mind was spinning so hard that she felt dizzy. So much had happened since the day Colonel Sprague had bought her. She perched herself on the windowsill, refreshed by the cool night breezes, and tried to figure it all out.

There were the runaways, for one thing. Did they believe all that stuff that Job had talked about? Did they know how to read and write? If freedom was coming anyway, why had they run away? It was certain that they had used the cave in their escape. Had the

Underground Railroad helped them, like Colonel Sprague said?

And what about Job? He had said that her name meant a flower that was supposed to grow free, and he had written it down on paper for her just like a white folk's name. Had he helped the field hands to escape? He was nowhere to be found early the next morning. Had he taken them to the cave? She did not dare ask him after Master's dreadful warning.

Then there were all the things he had said to her tonight, such as that whips and chains can enslave your body but not your mind. Now, how could part of a person be a slave and part be free? But none of these things were half as important as what Job had said about slavery not being the will of the Lord. She would have to do a powerful lot of thinking about that.

Cowslip started to crawl back through the nursery window, but she stopped suddenly, remembering Reba. When she left the cabin earlier, Reba had been suffering pitifully from the infection in her back, and her whole body had been burning up with fever. Dropping silently to the ground again, she raced down the moonlit hill to the white cabin.

The room was still when she entered, and

the figures of the sleeping women were strewn about the floor like bales of straw. Cowslip looked for Reba and found her asleep on the hard earth floor. Mehitabel sat beside her nodding wearily.

The old cook's eyes popped open wide as Cowslip came near. "Her fever's broke," Mehitabel whispered hoarsely. "She's going to be all right." Tenderly she swept a strand of hair from Reba's forehead and stretched out on the floor beside her.

Cowslip nodded and tiptoed to the fireplace, where the coals still gave off a soft red glow. She unfolded the paper and laid it in the warm ashes, tracing each letter with her finger. Over and over she followed the lines until she could close her eyes and see her name clearly written in her mind.

Finally she brushed the ashes off the paper and folded it again. It was late, and she was bone tired. Still, she knew that when she went back to the house, she would not be able to go to sleep. She crossed the room to where the old cook lay and called softly, "Mehitabel. Are you asleep?"

"No, girl. What is it?"

"That Job's a strange one. How come he knows so much?"

"Mercy me. Don't you know about Job?"

"I reckon not," Cowslip answered. Now she was more puzzled than ever. "What about him?"

"Why, girl, he's been free."

"Free!" Cowslip whistled softly in the dark. "Glory be!"

"I suppose you want to hear about it right now in the middle of the night," Mehitabel said in a half scolding voice.

Cowslip did not answer. How could she possibly go to sleep without knowing the story? Still, half the night was gone, and Mehitabel had spent long hours sitting beside Reba instead of resting herself.

"Of course I'm going to tell it to you now," Mehitabel added, and Cowslip could feel her warm smile through the darkness even though she could not see it. "You just scoot yourself over closer, so as we won't wake nobody up with our talking."

CHAPTER 11

"Long time ago," Mehitabel began, "Job belonged to a kind master. He let Job have a
wife, though the law said blacks couldn't
marry, and Job and his wife lived right in the
big house. They took real good care of Master
and his family.

"One night Master was away, and fire
broke out. Job saved Master's little child, but
when he went back for his own wife, the
flames had done took over.

"They say that when Master come back
and found out what happened, he set right
down and cried for Job's poor wife. Then he

told Job that he had done all that a human body could do for a master, and he set him free."

"A freedman!" Cowslip gasped.

"Yes, sirree, he was a freedman all right, with papers to prove it too. He marched hisself all the way to Philadelphia, where there's lots of free black folks. Some's freed like Job was, and some's runaways, but up north it's against the law for one person to own another, so everybody's free."

"Well, if he's got papers saying he's free, how come he's slaving now?" asked Cowslip. "It sure don't make much sense."

"Don't rush me, girl. I'm getting to that part."

Mehitabel shifted her giant frame slightly and bent down to check Reba before she went on.

"Job found work and started going to school at night. He took to schooling so good that before long he was teaching school his own self.

"Then one night two white men knocked on his door. They said, 'Boy, who's your master?' And Job said, 'I don't got no master. I've done been set free.' 'So let's see your papers to prove it,' they said. Job brung out his papers and them men grabbed them and burnt them to an ash. 'Now how you going to prove you're free?' they said, and they tied him up and carried him off and sold him down the river for a runaway. And that's how come he's slaving now and how come he's so smart."

Cowslip shuddered as she thought about Job. "It's bad enough always being a slave. It must be something awful to be a slave supposing you've ever once been free."

Free. *Free.* The word was all around her, and Job, whose room she had been in that very night, had once been free.

"Why, it sends tingles clean up my back to think that I've stood toe to toe to a freedman," she said.

But Mehitabel's only answer was deep, measured breathing. She was already asleep.

Cowslip hurried back to the big house. Job's window was dark now, and as she climbed back into the nursery and dropped into her bed, she tried to remember his face.

If he was really so special, wouldn't it show? Still, he had seemed different to her from the very first moment she had met him. Was it because he had been free?

She stretched out on her back and opened her eyes wide in the dark, trying with all her might to make his face appear. Mentally she tiptoed around corners in the big house and peered over rocks and under tree limbs outside, but each time she got close, his face ducked away from sight in her memory, the way a turtle pulls into its shell at the first hint of danger.

Everything about that man's an exasperation, she thought. He said that if your mind was free, you'd want your body to be free too. Then how come he takes slaving all so peaceful and quiet? How come he ain't raising Cain and trying to run away? There sure is a lot to figure out.

Cowslip awoke the next morning to the sound of the slave driver's horn. Even though she was in the big house and Tanner was off down the hill, blowing his horn as he rode his big chestnut horse around the slave cabins, it was the same kind of sound that had called her to work every day of her life that she could remember, and it tore away the heavy blanket of sleep that covered her.

She walked to the window and looked out at the hazy sky. The smell of rain was in the air. If only it would hold off for a while. She had promised the children a romp in the woods after breakfast, partly because they were always begging to play there and partly because she wanted to look around for a dead bird. She had to have it to lay the curse on Colonel Sprague. She was not sure just how she would get his name written down on a piece of paper, but one thing was certain, she would get it somehow.

Joel and Laura Margaret bounded out of bed and gobbled down their breakfast, eager to get started for the woods. Cowslip was eager too, and she hummed a little tune as she gathered Toby into her arms and herded the children down the stairs and out the back door.

"Race you down the hill," Joel shouted to his sister.

The two of them streaked off toward the bottom of the hill where the woods began. Cowslip meandered after them, bouncing Toby gently on her hip. She enjoyed having a few moments to herself just to smell the warm earth and taste the wind.

When the children darted in among the dense trees, she followed, and soon the strange events of the night before were forgotten as she happily joined them in a game of hide-and-seek. Cowslip was It, as usual, even though she could not count. She sat Toby down to play beside the log that was home base and hid her face in her hands for a moment while Joel and Laura Margaret scrambled to their hiding places.

Cowslip then looked this way and that, pretending not to see Laura Margaret standing behind a nearby tree. She was always easy to find because she did not like to get dirty. Joel, on the other hand, usually wriggled into the undergrowth and came out with cockleburs in his hair, dirt caked in his ears, and green stains from the grass all over his clothes.

Cowslip supposed it would take a while to locate Joel, but suddenly, from somewhere behind her, he raced to the log shouting, "Free! Free!"

"Free?" Cowslip screeched, startling both Joel and Laura Margaret, who was peeking out from her hiding place. "Is that the only word anyone on this plantation knows?"

Joel began to whimper, and instantly Cowslip felt ashamed. What had come over her? She had not meant to yell at the children.

Laura Margaret kept her eyes downcast as she tried without success to brush the dirt and leaves off Joel's clothes. When Cowslip started brushing too, Laura Margaret turned away.

"I know what. Let's play follow-the-leader," Cowslip suggested. "Laura Margaret, you be the leader and head off toward the washhouse. We surely can't take Joel back to the big house until he's cleaned up a smidgen."

Laura Margaret lit out through the woods,

with Joel right behind her. Over rocks and around trees they went. Cowslip sighed with relief, shifted Toby to the other hip, and followed them, keeping a sharp lookout for a dead bird as she went along.

Soon they came to the edge of the woods and saw smoke curling above the washhouse. Hag was outside taking bed linens off the line and grunting loudly as she worked.

"These things ain't ever going to dry today," she muttered to Cowslip. Then, seeing Joel, she began to cackle. "Well, if you're not the sorriest-looking sight I've seen in many a day."

Hag took Joel by the hand and led him into the washhouse. She perched him on top of the ironing board, poured hot water into a bowl, and began to scrub away the smudges. The steamy water and the fire in the stove made the washhouse unbearably hot, and Cowslip walked to the door to get some air. Looking toward the barn, she could see Job talking to Henry, the blacksmith, and the story Mehitabel had told her about Job the night before came rushing back.

"Hag," she said after a while, "did you know that Job's been free?"

"Sure. I reckon everybody knows about how he tried to live like white folks instead of the slave he was born." She paused to wipe her forehead with her apron and then went on, "Now I ask you, what good did it do him?"

"But he didn't just run away," Cowslip insisted. "His master set him free."

Hag pointed a bony finger at Cowslip. "The Lord puts temptation in everybody's path," she said. "You got to be *strong*. You got to know your place and stay in it."

Cowslip stared at the floor. How come those words didn't sound so right anymore? she wondered. She looked back up the hill. Henry was busy at his anvil, but Job was gone.

In bed that night, Cowslip argued with herself over what to do about the curse. One moment she wanted to go down to Job's room and ask him again to write down Master's name. Then another part of her was afraid that he would start in on her again about learning to read and write. Since she did not have a dead bird yet anyway, what was the use of getting the name in a hurry? Still, she argued back at herself, if she already had the name written down on paper when she found the bird, she would be all ready to lay the curse.

"Well, I ain't going to get no sleep just laying here and wrestling about it," she finally decided, and she got out of bed and quickly climbed down the tree.

Storm clouds had been threatening all evening. Now they gathered angrily overhead, hiding the moon. A strong wind swirled dust around her. It stung her eyes and made her want to cough, but she did not dare. One sound might bring Colonel Sprague or Tanner.

She was relieved to see that all the lights were out except Job's. The candle flickered on his windowsill exactly as it had the night before.

She crept close to the window and peered over the ledge. Job's chair was empty.

Just then a twig snapped behind her, and Cowslip whirled around. A knife of lightning split the air, and for an instant she saw the dark form of a man towering over her.

She took off at a run, her heart pounding wildly, as thunder rocked the ground beneath her. Big drops of rain smacked her as she ran, and then the cloudburst came. Sheets of rain battered her face. It soaked her thin dress and turned the bare earth into muddy rivers.

She slowed down once to look behind her. Her heart almost stopped. There he was, racing after her and waving his arms like a wind-tossed scarecrow.

Cowslip ran blindly, not knowing what direction she took. Too afraid to look back again, she zigzagged in and out of the woods and across the fields, desperately trying to lose her pursuer and succeeding, at the same time, in completely losing herself. Her legs were weak, and the sound of her own heavy breathing almost drowned out the noisy storm.

Just when she thought that she could go no farther, the outline of a building loomed ahead. It was almost as large as the main barn, but it stood far away from the big house and the other buildings of the plantation.

Must be one of the curing barns, she thought.

She struggled toward the building and fell against the side. Her eyes closed and she panted wildly as she waited for strength to come back into her legs.

Another bolt of lightning ripped across the sky, lighting up the night.

"I got to get inside before he finds me," she thought, pushing herself along the side of the barn until she came to the door. She lifted the latch and pulled the door open far enough to squeeze inside. With a surge of relief, she fell to her knees on the dry earthen floor. Then she heard the door swing shut again and the heavy outer latch fall into place. With a gasp, Cowslip shoved against the door as hard as she could. It would not budge. She was locked in.

CHAPTER 12

Cowslip sat very still, listening through the rain for the sound of footsteps. With each crash of thunder the picture of the man standing behind her in the dark flashed across her mind and made her tremble.

Who was he? What did he want? If he found her she was trapped because there was no other way out of the curing barn.

The building was used to dry the tobacco after harvest. It was empty now, but during curing season the leaves hung from frames over beds of hot coals. Smoke rose through the leaves, slowly drying and flavoring them.

The curing barns sat far away from the other buildings on the plantation, so that the heavy smoke would not blow too near the house. To make matters worse, no one came near them this time of year.

There were no windows, so Cowslip pressed her face against the door, trying to look out through the crack. All she could see was gray ribbons of rain whenever lightning illuminated the black night.

Suddenly her knees felt limp and a lump rose in her throat. What if he ain't a man, after all? she thought. What if he's the ghost of some poor tortured soul stalking around looking to find his rest?

Cowslip shuddered, remembering all the tales Mariah had told around the evening fire in the childhouse. She knew just about all that a living person could know about the spirit world, and she never let any of the children wander off to graveyards or lonely places, for fear they would run smack into a restless soul. The curing barn was just about the loneliest spot there was.

Mariah said that a body had to have a proper funeral or else he would never find his rest. His spirit would roam around forever, weeping and wailing and scaring folks half to death.

The air was cold, and Cowslip's wet dress stuck to her like frost. She shivered as she looked around for someplace to hide. Her eyes were getting used to the darkness, and she could see that the barn had been swept clean.

"There ain't no use to hide anyway. If he be a ghost, he'll walk right through them walls and find me sure."

This time she said the words out loud. The sound of her own voice made her feel less alone, so she crouched in a corner and hummed, but she hummed softly so that no one outside would hear her.

By morning the rain had stopped. Cowslip awoke to find herself still crumpled in the corner. Her sleep had been restless and full of frightening dreams, but at least the man or ghost or whatever he was had kept his distance. Now, with a splinter of sunlight coming in through the crack in the door, her terrible fears of the night before seemed foolish.

She stood up, brushing a thin crust of dried mud off her legs, and took a deep breath. The barn was already hot and steamy, and the heavy scent of tobacco hung thick and misty in the air.

"I'm going to be cured and ready for market my own self if I don't get out of this hot place pretty soon," she thought.

She ignored the gnawing in her stomach, because that only reminded her of how long it had been since she had eaten, and surveyed her prison. Perhaps she could find something in the daylight that she had not seen in the darkness. But everything looked the same.

She pushed against the door again, as if by some miracle the latch might have raised itself while she slept. It would not budge.

"Glory be," she thought. "What am I going to do?"

It was well after sunup, and by this time everyone on the plantation must know that she was missing. Colonel Sprague probably thought that she had run away and, at this very moment, might be forming search parties to track her down. There was not much doubt about the trouble she would be in when she was found.

She tilted her head sideways and tried to use both eyes to see through the crack in the door. It was not much better than using the eye. The crack was narrow, and all that she could make out was dark earth and blue sky.

Cowslip knew that somebody would take care of the children. Master would probably have one of the other house slaves look after them. Still, she could not help worrying. It might take days for someone to find her.

She licked her dry lips and began to tap on the walls of the barn. They were sturdy, but there was always a chance that one board might be loose. The heat burned her nostrils and made her dizzy, but she stubbornly pounded and pushed against each board.

Finally she gave up. Sinking to her knees, she rubbed her fingers across a sweating arm, gathering the precious moisture and patting it onto her lips.

"I suppose there ain't no use to holler for help," she thought. "But it's the only thing I ain't already tried."

She took a deep breath, cupped her hands around her mouth, and yelled, "Help! Help! Can anybody hear me?"

There was no answer except the faint echo of her own voice in the empty barn.

"Hello, out there! I'm locked in the barn and I can't get out!"

Even the wind was still, and Cowslip knew that no one was close enough to hear her. She fingered the hem of her dress for a moment or two and then she began to shout again.

"Colonel Sprague! You're meaner than a whip snake and uglier than a horned toad!"

Sitting back, she smiled with satisfaction,

but her dry throat was begining to ache, and she closed her eyes to keep the brimming tears from rushing down her cheeks.

"Job's the cause of all my troubles," she thought aloud. "Him and his high-toned talk of being free. He's got a lot of fancy words to match his fancy clothes, but all it done was get me in a peck of trouble. I ain't going to listen to him *no more!*"

Absently her finger scratched the loose dirt floor.

"I'd bet a passel that he's the one that stirred up Percy and the others to run away," she muttered. "And now he's working on me. Well, when Colonel Sprague finds me, I'll be anything but free. I'll likely wish that I was dead."

She pulled the bandanna off her head and frowned at it. "He said a cowslip is a flower that's growing wild and free. A lot of hogwash is what that is." She mopped her face with the yellow cloth and fanned with it for a moment before she tied it loosely over her hair once more.

She stretched her legs out straight in front of her and listened to the distant song of a bird, but still there was no human sound to be heard. The hot air pressed down so heavily that it did not seem worthwhile to move any farther. She fixed her gaze on the door and wished for somebody — anybody — to open it.

Then, for an instant, she thought she heard someone gently patting the ground outside the barn. She shook herself to be sure that she was awake, and listened. The sound grew stronger. Suddenly she knew that it was feet instead of hands — running feet, slapping against the earth. She held her breath and listened as they came nearer and nearer to the barn.

Cowslip staggered to her feet and stumbled toward the door. "Help! Get me out of here! Help! Help!" she shouted, her voice coming out hoarse from her parched throat.

She held her breath and listened for an answer. None came. Even the footsteps had stopped, and silence hung around her as thick as smoke.

"Please help me," she sobbed, pounding on the door. "I'm locked in. I can't get out."

She flattened her ear against the slit in the door and strained to hear the smallest sound. Finally she sank to the floor and closed her eyes.

She sat there, numb with disappointment, for a long time before the ghostly fears crept back into her mind.

"I know I heard somebody," she thought. "How come he got so quiet?"

She opened her eyes as wide as she could and slowly peered around at the shadows in the barn. "I was right. He ain't a regular person or else he'd come and let me out. He's a ghost. Or worse yet . . . maybe he's a plat-eye!"

The worst kind of ghosts were plat-eyes. Mariah had said that they were spirits of poor unfortunates who had died unnatural deaths, and they would harm any living creature that they met.

Plat-eyes did not look like the humans they had once been. Instead, they could take any form they wanted to and could change from one shape to another as quick as you please. Sometimes they stalked the earth as animals; other times they floated around like swamp gas and suffocated anybody who came their way. A headless man was sure to be a plat-eye, and so was a snake with two tails.

Cowslip had never seen a ghost. All the same, she had heard enough about the ways of spirits to know that if the footsteps she had heard were those of a plat-eye, she would never get out of the curing barn alive.

The footsteps sounded again. They were softer and slower this time, like tiptoeing, but they were coming straight toward the barn.

"I reckon the Lord is punishing me for questioning His will," she thought. She stood dizzily and faced the door.

CHAPTER 13

The footsteps outside came to a stop. Cowslip
stiffened. Man or ghost, he was directly in
front of her now. Only the barn door stood
between them.

"Cowslip?"

The small voice was squeaky with fright.

"Joel!" she cried. "Joel, is that you?"

"Uh-huh."

His answer was more a sigh than a word,
and Cowslip realized that he had been just as
much afraid of the voice coming from inside

130

the barn as she had been of the mysterious footsteps outside.

"What are you doing so far away from the big house?" she demanded. "Did you run off again?"

Joel did not answer. There was only silence for a moment, and then suddenly Cowslip heard footsteps again. This time they were running away from the barn.

"Joel!" she shrieked. "Come back here."

When the sound of her voice had died away, the footsteps were gone too. She could not be sure whether Joel had stopped or was too far away to be heard.

"Joel," she called. "I won't whip you for running off. I promise I won't. Just help me get out of this barn."

Cowslip held her breath and waited. There was a long silence, but finally she could hear the soft crunching of dirt underfoot. Joel was coming back.

He bumped and banged against the door for a moment and then said in a timid voice, "I'm too little. I can't reach the latch."

"Is there anything outside to stand on?"

"Nope."

"Well, how about a big stick or board that you could push the latch up with?"

"Nope."

"Well, ain't there nothing out there at all?"

"Nope. Nothing."

Cowslip sighed and sat down on the dirt floor to think. There was just one thing to do.

"Joel," she said softly. "You hightail it back to the big house and fetch help. Do you hear?"

"Nope."

"What do you mean, nope? I got to get out of here or else I'll die."

"I'd get whipped for coming down here by myself."

"I done told you, I ain't going to whip you for running off this time."

"My papa would, though," he answered solemnly. "Besides, he thinks you ran away and he's giving a big reward to anybody who catches you."

"Would he give the reward to you?" she asked hopefully.

Joel was silent for a while.

"Nope," he said at last and took off at a run. Cowslip listened as his footsteps grew fainter and fainter until she could no longer hear them.

"If they think I run off, they won't be looking for me anywhere on the plantation," she thought. "That means the only other hope I got is whoever it was that chased me last night, and I don't know if he's a man or a ghost or what he'll do when he finds me. Glory be," she whispered. "If I ever get out of..."

Her words trailed off into silence as she noticed the spot where she had been sitting all through the morning. There, scrawled over and over in the dirt, was her name.

Cowslip stared at the letters. When had she written them? The same sense of awe swept over her that she had felt when she first saw Job write them on the slate. But this time her awe was mixed with anger.

"That was a stupid thing to do," she said to herself. She scooted across the floor and quickly brushed away the words with her hand. "He taught me to write just so I'd spend my days wishing to be what I ain't. Well, I won't do it. I'll show him. I just won't do it!"

She did not try to hold back the tears this time. Stretched out on the barn floor, her body shook with sobs and her tears made mud blobs in the dust.

A long time later she felt the gentle nudging of a hand upon her shoulder.

"Cowslip. Wake up," said a soft voice.

She opened her eyes and squinted into the bright light that was streaming through the open door. It was Job, and Joel stood by his side. She reached for Joel and hugged him tightly.

"Glory be," she whispered. "Glory be."

She was weak from hunger and from the heat, so they walked back toward the big house slowly, stopping often so that she could rest. Joel bobbed along a good distance in front of them, tossing pebbles into the air that now and then landed on his own small head.

Cowslip was silent. She almost would have preferred that Colonel Sprague had come after her himself instead of Job. She snatched quick glances at him from the corner of her eye as he strode along importantly, looking neither to one side nor the other.

Finally, when Joel had spurted far ahead and could not hear, Job turned to her and said, "I'm sorry that I frightened you last night."

"You mean you was the one that scared me half to death?" Cowslip gasped.

Job nodded. "I tried to call to you, to tell you it was me, but the storm was so loud that you couldn't hear me above it. Then I tried to catch you, but I lost you in the darkness. Why were you coming to see me?"

"I wasn't," she answered tensely.

"Were you coming to tell me that you're ready to learn to read and write?"

"No," she blurted out. "I was just going for a walk. That's all."

"Please promise me one thing," he said. "Colonel Sprague must never know that I left my room last night. I can't tell you why right now. Just trust me."

Cowslip could not believe it. All the time she had been trapped in the curing barn — hungry, thirsty, afraid — it had been on account of Job. Now she would have to explain to Colonel Sprague what she had been doing there, and Job had the gall to ask her for help. Well, maybe she would just tell Colonel Sprague about Job going places in the night and about the slate he had hidden in his room and how he could read and write and believed that blacks ought to be free. That would put an end to his troublemaking once and for all. Still, the nearer they got to the big house, the more she dreaded facing Colonel Sprague.

"I'll just have to do it," she thought, "and take whatever punishment he gives me. I surely have learned my lesson."

Job sprang to open the door in butler fashion and gestured for her to enter first. She could see Colonel Sprague in the library, bent over his desk in deep concentration. She straightened her yellow bandanna and walked slowly and soundlessly across the soft carpet. Biting hard on her lower lip to keep it from quivering, she stopped in front of the desk. Colonel Sprague was writing something on a sheet of paper with a quill the color of blood and he did not see her standing there.

Cowslip gazed from one side of the room to the other. All she could see was books. They lined the walls from ceiling to floor, with gaps only for the fireplace and the door.

"How many words in all them books?" she wondered. "I'll bet Job can read all of them."

Suddenly her empty stomach growled, and Colonel Sprague sprang upright in his chair. His eyes held their startled expression for only an instant before they hardened into rage.

"Cowslip!" he thundered. His fist crashed down upon the desk, tossing papers helter-skelter onto the floor. "Where have you been?"

Before she could answer, a frightened cry pierced the air. It was Toby, wailing pitifully from the nursery above.

Colonel Sprague cast his gaze toward the ceiling and looked for a moment as if he were angry enough to go right through it. Then he sighed heavily and glared at Cowslip.

"Well?" His voice was loud and furious.

Cowslip wondered if Job was listening outside the library door. How could he expect her to figure out what to say? What would he do if she decided to tell Colonel Sprague the truth?

"Well, Colonel Sprague, sir," she began slowly. She paused, listening for some sound of Job, but all she could hear was Toby's shrieks.

"I guess I must have been walking in my sleep," she offered in a shaky voice. Colonel Sprague was frowning in disbelief, so she rushed on, letting the words tumble out. "I woke up when I got outside, but just then the storm broke. It gave me such a fright I took off running. I didn't stop until I came to this here building, and I ran inside and the door latched behind me, locking me in, and I'd be right now dying of hunger and thirst if Joel hadn't found me."

Colonel Sprague raised his eyebrows at the sound of his son's name.

"I promised Joel he would't get whipped for going so far alone if he'd just go for help," Cowslip added quickly.

"Oh, you did, did you?" the Colonel blustered.

Above them, Toby let out another howl.

"Run upstairs and quiet Toby while I decide how I'm going to punish you," he ordered.

"And you get right back down here as soon as he's asleep."

Cowslip raced up the stairs and into the nursery, where Chloella was pacing the floor with Toby in her arms. Laura Margaret sat forlornly in one corner, but the moment she saw Cowslip, she ran to her and gave her a hug. And by the time Cowslip took Toby in her arms, there was a smile on his tear-streaked face and he was rubbing his sleepy eyes with a fat little fist.

"They ain't no gladder to see you than I am," said Chloella as she hurried out of the nursery.

A few minutes later Cowslip returned to the library.

"I ought to whip you," Colonel Sprague said grimly. His glance flickered toward the ceiling. "But I won't. You're the only one who can keep peace and quiet in this house while my wife is away. Instead, I have something more appropriate in mind."

He rose and headed for the door.

"Come along," he said.

Master led her out of the house and across the barn lot, not stopping until they reached the spot where Henry, the colored blacksmith, stood.

"Fit her with a neck iron," the Colonel growled, and disappeared into the barn.

Henry shook his head sadly. "I'll be easy as I can," he said.

Cowslip nodded and gritted her teeth, standing straight and still while Henry slipped one cold metal collar after another around her neck until he found one that fit.

Colonel Sprague reappeared, and he was carrying something in his hand.

"This is the second time that you were found in a place where you had no business being. Do you know what they do to cattle that insist on straying?" he asked angrily.

Cowslip stiffened and looked at the object in his hand. It was a bell.

"Here," the Colonel said, handing the bell to the blacksmith. "Put this on her neck iron."

Turning, he strode back toward the house.

Cowslip felt weak and sick with shame. She wanted to crawl away into the bushes like a hurt animal and die. She hardly felt the heat of the forge and the jerks and clanks as Henry fastened on the bell.

Suddenly Job's words came back to her. "Master takes every precaution to keep his slaves as mindless as a flock of chickens," Job had said. "To him they're animals, and they come to think of themselves as animals too."

Cowslip spun around in time to see Colonel Sprague cross the porch of the big house and walk through the door and out of sight.

Her face contorted with helpless fury. *I ain't no animal!* she wanted to shout. Just in time she was able to hold her tongue. She could not risk a whipping too.

Her yellow bandanna had fallen off her head and lay at her feet. She looked down at it thoughtfully.

"But then, I ain't no flower, neither . . . . I'm *me!*"

CHAPTER 14

The heavy bell clanked rudely every time Cowslip moved. She put one hand over the clapper and shuffled toward the summer kitchen. It was almost dark, and the other house slaves would surely be inside eating their evening meal. How could she face them clanking like a stray goat?

She leaned against the corner of the big house for a moment, watching the last scarlet fingers of sunlight slip down behind the hills. The afternoon had been a nightmare. Trying to keep the bell from frightening Toby had been hard enough, and Joel's giggling and pointing had not been much better. But the way Laura Margaret had stared solemnly at it, unable to pull her tear-filled eyes away, had been harder than anything.

Finally, Cowslip walked into the summer kitchen and stood stiffly facing the others as if she were standing on the auction block again. The room grew silent. She stared at the corner of the table, not looking at anybody, but she could feel the anguish in their eyes.

They're all weighing it and feeling it around their own necks, she thought. But there's a sight more to wearing it than they'll ever know.

A few of the women stirred, but still no one spoke. Then, all at once, someone started to laugh. Cowslip saw with disbelief that it was Mehitabel and that she had gotten up and was coming toward her rocking with mirth.

"If that fancy necklace you're wearing don't beat all," she chortled, slapping her big thighs.

Cowslip's mouth dropped open. Surely she had heard wrong; surely she did not see Mehitabel laughing.

Nevertheless, Mehitabel stood before her, a broad grin lighting up her face, and now some of the other women were laughing too.

"It ain't funny!" Cowslip shrieked. "Don't you laugh at me."

Slowly Cowslip dropped to her knees. The

tears flowed down her cheeks, and she did not even notice when Mehitabel sank to the floor beside her. Mehitabel clasped Cowslip's small hands inside her own.

"Mercy, girl. Hush," she said. Her voice was almost a moan. "I surely thought you knew about laughing."

Cowslip stared into her lap. What did Mehitabel mean? Of course she knew about laughing. Mostly it was being happy, but sometimes it was making fun. She did not want to answer Mehitabel or to look into the face that she had once trusted.

"You see," Mehitabel said softly, "sometimes white folks try to kill the very soul of blacks by making them feel ashamed and no account. And laughing . . . well, laughing is like a blanket that cozies up your poor bare soul and keeps it safe from harm."

Slowly Cowslip raised her eyes. Mehitabel's gaze was full of love. She was not laughing now.

"It's all right that you didn't know, because it's a black secret that's guarded well. White folks don't realize that the reason we laugh is because we know that trouble don't last forever and that the worse things get, the sooner they got to get better. Why, they think we laugh because we're simple in the head."

With this Mehitabel began to chuckle again, and Cowslip could not help but smile.

"That's just what they're supposed to think," Mehitabel said. Then her face clouded into a frown, and the words that followed were slow and measured. "But our laughing and our Lord is all we got."

The room grew silent again, and a look of sorrow spread across the women's faces. Slowly they returned to their supper, and Reba, who was eating in the summer kitchen for the first time since her whipping, beckoned to Cowslip.

Cowslip sat down beside her, but she was too miserable to eat.

"I got something for you," Reba said with a smile. Reaching to the waistband of her skirt, she pulled out the white handkerchief edged with lace that she always kept with her. She wrapped it around and around the clapper of Cowslip's bell and tied it securely.

"There," Reba said with pride. "You won't be able to wear that during the day when Master is around, but at least at night you can have some peace and quiet."

Cowslip opened her mouth to say thank you, but Reba shook her head.

"My Percy would want you to have it too," she said. "He found it beside the road once when Master sent him to fetch old Doc. Because it's got fancy lace on it, he said it was to be a sign that we was trothed. But right now it'll do you a heap more good than me."

"It's a mighty special thing to part with," Cowslip said. "I'll take the best care of it I can so's you can have it back as soon as Master takes off this bell."

Reba gave Cowslip's hand a warm squeeze in reply, and the two girls lapsed into silence, each one deep in thoughts of her own.

It had seemed like an endless day, and Cowslip's shoulders ached from the weight around her neck. She tiptoed to the back door of the big house and quickly looked into the dining room. Laura Margaret and Joel were still eating supper with their father. She would have a few more minutes to herself.

Back outside, Cowslip headed for the giant oak tree that had been her stairway out of the nursery and straight into trouble. It was one of the biggest trees on the plantation, and she and Joel and Laura Margaret could barely join hands around it. Sitting down among the sprawling roots, she leaned against the trunk and closed her eyes, aware of nothing but the tiredness ebbing from her aching arms and legs.

She was almost asleep when the sound of

Reba's voice pushed through the drowsy haze that filled her mind. "Cowslip. Is something wrong?"

"No," she whispered.

Reba sighed and sat down beside her. Overhead the stars twinkled brightly, and a soft breeze rustled the leaves.

"Sure is peaceful out here," murmured Reba.

"Sure is," Cowslip said. "Wish I was as peaceful inside me."

"What do you mean?" asked Reba.

"Well, back on the old plantation, Mariah said black folks got to get revenge. Now that I'm here, Hag says I got to know my place. Master says I got to be an animal. Job says I got to know things I ain't supposed to know, and Mehitabel says I got to laugh. Ain't there no way I can just be me?"

Reba did not answer.

"Well, if there ain't, what's the use of living anyway?"

"Cowslip! Don't you never talk that way. You come north to Canada with me and Percy. Nobody up there'll tell you how you got to be."

"I can't just run away."

"Why not?"

"Because I was born a slave, and this is where I belong. Leastways, I think it is. I just got to find some way to be myself and be Master's slave girl too."

Reba shook her head. "Take my word. You ain't never going to find a way to do that. You're just going to have to decide which you want to be the most." She laughed softly, rose, and started walking down the hill toward the white cabin.

"If you change your mind, you'd be mighty welcome to come along," she called softly over her shoulder.

Cowslip watched Reba until she disappeared in the shadows.

"Now Reba says I got to run away. Lordy, Lordy. How am I going to know what's right for me?" Cowslip said to herself.

Cowslip laid her head back against the tree and curled her legs beneath her. The heavy pull of the bell made her feel more tired than she already was. Then her hand brushed the grass and rested on something small and soft. She picked it up and examined it in the moonlight.

"Glory be," she thought. "The Lord done sent his answer to me sure."

CHAPTER 15

"The Lord and hoodoo curses don't go together, girl," Job said sternly as he parted the handful of leaves that Cowslip had given him and looked at the dead sparrow inside. "In the first place, curses don't work."

Cowslip frowned. Of course they worked. Mariah would not have said so unless it was true. Besides, she had seen a curse work with her very own eyes.

"Curses are just foolish hopes dreamed up by folks who don't know any other way to get revenge," Job said solemnly. "And the Lord only turns His mighty hand for the cause of good."

Cowslip looked down at her toes. Why was

it that every time she came to Job for help he turned things around backward and made her wish that she had never come?

"But I suppose if it's the only way to get you to learn to read and write, we'll have to give your curse a try," he added with a smile.

Job placed the small gray bird and its shroud of leaves on the winddowsill and drew his slate and a piece of chalk from behind the bed. He broke the chalk in half, handing one piece to Cowslip.

"If we're going to have school," he said, "we'll have to do it in the proper way. First, you must learn to write your name across the top of the slate, just as I wrote if for you when you came to see me before. Here, I'll show you again."

Job reached for the slate, but Cowslip was quicker. She plopped it onto her lap, clasped the chalk firmly with her fingers, and began to write.

COWSLIP

Beaming triumphantly, she turned the slate around for Job to see.

"Now teach me to write Colonel Sprague's name," she urged.

Job nodded his approval and took the slate. "Well now, as quickly as you learn, we'll have you reading and writing in no time."

Cowslip dropped to her knees beside him and watched tensely as he began to make letters.

COLONEL SPRAGUE

Job handed the slate back to her. "Now you copy the letters underneath the ones I made."

Cowslip sat very still for a moment, looking at her master's name. "White folks even got bigger names than blacks," she mused. "But that don't surprise me none."

She went right to work at her task. Most of the letters were new to her and hard to make, but she wrote them over and over, erasing them with the hem of her dress and writing them again until her fingers cramped.

Job watched every letter that she made, helping her here, correcting her there. At last he stood up and went to the door.

"I think you're ready," he said, and motioned for her to be still. "Come with me."

Without another word, he slipped into the dark hallway. She took a deep breath and followed him. Where was he going? One small sound might bring the Colonel. Slowly she inched a hand upward until she grasped the clapper of her bell. Even wrapped in Reba's handkerchief, it clanked dully whenever she moved. She pressed the other hand against Job's back to keep from losing him in the darkness.

The floorboards squeaked beneath the carpet, and Cowslip silently prayed that Master was fast asleep.

She could see nothing through the blackness, but she felt Job turn, and her arm scraped against a door frame. Were they going into a room? An instant later the latch clicked softly behind them.

"I'll light a lamp," Job whispered.

In the flare of the match, Cowslip saw that they were in the library, and in another moment the lamp had spread its light across the rows and rows of books that filled the room.

Job took her by the arm and gently led her to the black leather chair that stood behind the Colonel's huge oak desk.

"Sit down," he urged. Seeing her hesitate, he added, "It's all right. No one will know."

The chair was soft and deep, and when she sank into it, her feet no longer touched the floor.

Job put a piece of paper on the desk in front of her. Then he picked up a quill pen with an enormous scarlet plume, dipped it into the ink pot, and handed it to her.

Cowslip gasped. It was the very quill that Colonel Sprague had been using when she stood before him earlier in the day.

"It's only right that you should use Master's own pen to cast your spell on him," Job said.

Cowslip took the pen with a trembling hand. Glancing quickly around the booklined room, she began to write.

COLONEL

She dipped the pen into the ink again.

SPRAGU

She filled the quill for the last time. Only one more letter, and revenge against Master would surely be hers.

E

There. It was done.

Cowslip stared at the pen, watching a blob of ink drop onto the paper, almost covering the E that she had just made. She did not want to give it back, but Job was holding out his hand insistently.

Her eyes were on the pen again. She felt its weight and looked at it in her hand.

"Glory be," she whispered, handing it back to Job at last. "Glory be."

Silently they crept back to Job's room. She folded the paper and placed it in the dead sparrow's beak just as Mariah had said it must be done. When she slipped out through the window, she put the bird behind a honeysuckle bush near the door to the summer kitchen, where she could check it every evening. Then she climbed back up the oak tree to the nursery and fell quickly to sleep, too exhausted to dream.

In the weeks that followed, Cowslip began learning to read and write. At night, in Job's tiny room, she placed the precious slate across her lap, clasped the chalk firmly, and wrote her name. After that, the lesson began.

Most of the time she labored over the "three R's" as Job told her they were called. But sometimes, on very special nights, Job just talked. He told her about the world outside the plantation, the world of free men and women, and about the Underground Railroad.

"I help to run it through this part of Kentucky," he confided to her one night. "And I can start any slave on the road to freedom if he's of a mind to go."

Cowslip stared at him in disbelief.

"Remember the night I frightened you outside my window?" he asked.

Cowslip nodded. How could she forget?

"That night I passed along a field hand from Arkansas to a white man that runs a boat up and down the Mississippi River. I was on my way back to my room when you saw me. Now you know why Colonel Sprague must never find out that I sometimes leave this room at night."

"I can't believe so many'd help to free black folks," said Cowslip. "Especially whites. Why do they care about us anyway?"

"Because they know that we're human beings and that every human being should be free."

She thought about what he was saying for a moment, weighing it in her mind. But there was still one thing that puzzled her. "If being free is so good, why don't you escape on the Underground Railroad your own self instead of helping everybody else?"

Job's face grew solemn. "I've already had my taste of freedom," he said quietly. "And if I ran away I'd take away the chance for a lot of other folks to be free too... maybe even you."

Cowslip looked quickly at her feet. She did not want to think about that now. Maybe later, when she was not so afraid, she would think about it, but not right now.

The next morning at breakfast Mehitabel was as flappy as a goose.

"Mistress is coming home tomorrow," she announced excitedly. "We got to put a shine on this house and everything in it."

Joel and Laura Margaret danced around the kitchen singing, "Mamma's coming home.

Mamma's coming home," at the top of their voices. Cowslip was pleased too. She had liked Mistress, even though she was a white woman, and had been secretly hoping that she would be able to keep her job minding the children even after Mrs. Sprague returned.

Mehitabel shooed everyone out as soon as breakfast was over, and she and Reba set to work cleaning every nook and cranny of the kitchen. Sarah and Chloella turned the rest of the house inside out, making it sparkle, and Job polished the silver and set bowls of freshly cut roses in every room. But no one worked harder than Cowslip. By the end of the day, there was not a toy out of place in the nursery, nor a piece of clothing in need of mending. The floors and windows shone, and the children were scrubbed pink before they tumbled into bed.

Cowslip was exhausted. She looked nervously around the nursery. It was as clean and neat as she could make it, but what if that wasn't enough? What if Mistress did not want her to tend the young'uns anymore? What if this was her last night in the big house? Maybe tomorrow she would be a field hand and live off down the hill in one of the cabins. If that happened, how would she get to see Job? There was so much for her to learn, and there was one thing in particular that she just had to know. If this was to be her last night in the big house, she would have to find out about it tonight.

She shinnied down the tree and slipped into Job's room as usual, but she shook her head when he offered her the slate.

"Tonight I want to read," she said.

"All right, I'll write some words on the slate for you."

"No. I want to read out of the Bible. I want to see for my own self that part that says blacks always got to be slaves, just like you said I should."

Job stood still, regarding her thoughtfully for a moment. Finally he nodded. There was a sad look in his eyes, and Cowslip thought he seemed extra tired as he slowly left the room. Soon he was back with the Master's leather-bound Bible in his hand. He opened it to a page near the front of the book and squinted at the words for an instant until he found the place.

"Genesis: Chapter nine; verses nineteen through twenty-five," he said softly, pointing to a line on the page. "Start reading here."

" 'These — these are the — three — sons — of Noah,' " she began haltingly.

Slowly she read down the page, with Job helping her more often than not. The words were hard to read and Cowslip did not know many of them by sight, but they were words she had heard so many times before that she had almost memorized them. When she reached the last line, tears streamed down her face and her voice was barely a whisper.

" 'And he said — Cursed — be Canaan — a servant of servants — shall he be — unto his — brethren.' "

Cowslip let the book fall to the bed, and the pages closed with a loud slap.

"How can it say that?" she sobbed. "You're supposed to know so much. Tell me why it says them words."

She grabbed Job's hand, looking up at him with pleading eyes. Surely he would know the answer. He was the one who had given her hope in the first place. He wouldn't take it away again like this.

He sighed deeply and sat down on the bed beside her. "I'd give anything to be able to explain it, child, but I cannot. I know that it's not much help to say that many of the Lord's words are beyond our understanding and that maybe someday smarter men than I'll ever be will figure it out. But, Cowslip, some things I *do* know, and you know them too."

Job put his hand under Cowslip's chin and raised her face until her eyes met his. The look of sadness that she had seen a moment ago was gone. Now they blazed liked twin candles in the night.

"I know that I am a man. I stand up straight on two legs. I laugh, I cry, and, most of all, I think. And a man — a man has got to be free! I *know* that, just the same way you know that you should never have to wear a bell around your neck!"

Cowslip sat rigidly still, held by his flaming eyes, trying to grasp the meaning of his words.

Then, suddenly, there was a loud pounding on the front door of the house.

"Colonel Sprague!"

It was Tanner, and his voice was wild with rage.

"Come quick. They're trying to escape!"

CHAPTER 16

"Go quickly. I have to let him in," Job whispered.

Cowslip flattened herself against the wall as Job jerked open the door and rushed into the hall. When the door fanned open, the flame on the windowsill blew out, and she stood alone in the darkness, paralyzed with fear.

What if she were found? She could not stay in Job's room any longer.

Her legs were shaking as she tiptoed toward the window. Slowly she crawled out, stretching her toes downward to find the soft ground below. Suddenly her bell clanked against the wooden sill. Her stomach tightened, but the noise she had made was lost in a second burst of hammering on the front door.

Cowslip started to climb back up the tree to the safety of the nursery, but lamps were going on all over the big house, shooting streams of light all around her. She ducked into the shadows and made her way carefully toward the white cabin. She would wait there until the commotion died down, and pray that the children would not awaken and need her.

Mehitabel met her at the door. A worried frown creased her face.

"I thought it was them coming back," she said in a hoarse whisper.

"Who?"

"Reba and Percy."

With a sweeping glance Cowslip looked around the room at the sleeping forms strewn across the floor. Reba was not among them.

"You mean . . . you mean he come for her?"

"Yes, all by hisself, just like he said he would. They ain't been gone but just a few minutes."

Cowslip's thoughts raced to the runaways. Tanner knew that someone was trying to escape, and he would be going after them any minute. Where had they gone?

The cave! Percy didn't need Job's help to find the cave; he had been there once before. But what he didn't know was that Master had been there too.

"I got to warn them," she mumbled, brushing past Mehitabel and racing back into the night.

Even if there had been time, she could not get to Job with Master out of bed and Tanner in the house. She would have to go alone and pray that she would be in time.

She stopped outside the cabin to get her bearings. The moon was almost full, and its white light covered the countryside like frost. She could not chance using the road. Instead, her route lay dangerously close to the big house. She pulled the yellow bandanna off her head and wadded it up in her hand so that it would not be seen in the brightness of the moonlight and give her away. Perhaps if she moved slowly and blended into the shadows, no one would notice her.

Crouching low and holding her breath, she crept up the hill and into the sprawling backyard. Lights glowed from many windows, and she could hear a horse, probably Tanner's, stomping and snorting his impatience to be off on the search as he waited near the front door.

The back of the house was quiet, and Cowslip stopped for a moment. Her knees were weak, and blood throbbed inside her head as she rested in the last refuge of darkness. In front of her was the moon-drenched lawn, melting into meadow. She could not hide again until she reached the other side, where the scrub pine and brambles grew along the rocky riverbank.

"I got to put my scaredness under my feet and stand on it," she whispered resolutely to herself.

Cowslip thrust herself forward, dashing down the dewy hill. Far behind her, along the road, the thunder of horses' hooves burst upon the silence and pounded in time with her pulse.

The bell thumped painfully against her chest as she gasped to get her breath while her legs churned faster and faster on the downhill slope. She could barely stay upright, but still, she knew, the Colonel's horse was faster.

Just ahead was the fringe of woods. Another moment or two, and she would reach the cave.

Cowslip stopped running and listened for

horses, but now only the sound of crickets pulsed against the night.

Glory be. I just can't be too late. I just can't!

All at once, rifle shots ripped the air. One. Two. Three shots. And then silence.

Cowslip stopped. Even the crickets were still. She sank to her knees, staring at the spot only a few feet away that was the entrance to the cave. Tied nearby were two saddled horses. One was the prize black stallion that belonged to Colonel Sprague. The other was Tanner's chestnut mare.

One by one the crickets resumed their chirping. The threat of danger was past for them.

Reba and Percy were dead. The knowledge churned over and over in Cowslip's mind. She had not believed that Percy would come back for Reba. It had seemed impossible that he could make it all the way to Canada without getting caught and then come back for her. But he had come, and now Reba was gone, not to the better life she had dreamed of but to her death.

Cowslip struggled to her feet. There was no use staying here any longer.

She heard voices and looked up to see the Colonel and Tanner coming out of the cave carrying a shapeless form. They did not see her standing in the shadows, and she watched grimly as they lifted the body across the rump of the Colonel's horse. They returned to the cave and came out a moment later carrying a second body. Finally they brought out a third one, which they placed along with the second one across the back of Tanner's horse. After the bodies were secured, the two men mounted their overburdened horses and rode away.

Cowslip smoothed the yellow bandanna, which she was still clutching in her hand, and tied it around her head. It scarcely mattered now if someone saw her. Numb with grief, she trudged up the hillside toward the big house.

It wasn't fair, she thought. Reba was just a scared little slave girl who had never hurt anybody in her whole life. Why did he have to kill her?

Cowslip knew the answer. The Colonel had said it himself that day outside the cave. He had said that he would make such examples of Percy and the other runaways that no slave of his would ever try to escape again.

Surely slavery wasn't the will of the Lord, she thought, if masters had to do such terrible things to keep their slaves, and if folks like Reba and Percy and Job were willing to take such chances to get freedom for themselves and for other blacks.

Job. She stopped, remembering suddenly that there had been three bodies instead of only two. Mehitabel had said that Percy had come back for Reba by himself. Was the third body Job's? Had he found out somehow that Percy was here and gone to the cave to warn him and Reba, getting there ahead of the Master and Tanner but too late to save them?

Cowslip tried to run up the sloping meadow toward the big house, but her tired legs felt as heavy as logs, and she was barely able to drag them up the hill.

What if the other corpse was Job? What would she do? He must not desert her now.

At the edge of the lawn she knew she could go no farther, and she sank down in the grass to catch her breath. Stretching out on her back, Cowslip looked up at the sky. Her weary arms and legs felt as if they were floating up to meet the moon, which shone as brightly as if this night were just the same as any other night. . . .

But she could not lie here forever. She had to find out if Job was dead or alive. She pushed herself away from the ground and stood up and, drawing a long deep breath, started toward the big house again. It was not far now. Just a little more and she would be there.

No candle shone in Job's window, and the closer Cowslip came to it, the more afraid she was that he was dead. She tiptoed over and raised herself up slowly until she could see over the sill. Moonlight splashed across the floor and over the empty bed, but the single straight-backed chair was not empty. Job sat in it with his head buried in his hands.

"Glory be," she whispered. "He's alive."

She wanted to tap on the window and talk to him about what had happened and tell him how glad she was that at least he was alive, but there was no time. The promise of dawn was already painting the whole backyard a dismal gray. Tanner would be outside with the first pink rays of the sun, blowing the horn that called the slaves to work.

Cowslip pulled herself up the tree, hand over hand, until she finally rested on the nursery windowsill. She dropped silently into the room and saw with relief that the children all slept soundly.

She sat down on the edge of her bed, knowing that there was no use to lie down with dawn so near. Troubled thoughts swarmed around inside her head like gnats.

Who could that third body be? she wondered over and over again. Reba had once tried to persuade her to go up north with them. Had she found someone else who wanted to go? Still, Mehitabel had spoken only of Reba and Percy.

Glory be. Who could it be? The question pounded in Cowslip's head.

CHAPTER 17

Grief hung as black and heavy as funeral drapings around the house slaves' breakfast table that morning, where Reba's empty chair stood as a mute reminder of the tragedy of the night before.

Cowslip was the last to come into the kitchen. She pushed Joel and Laura Margaret toward the dining room to have breakfast with their father and busied herself feeding Toby before she joined the women at the table. The usual morning chatter was missing, and the only sound came from Toby, who blabbered contentedly in his high chair while he chewed on a crust of bread.

Finally, Job hurried in from the dining

room, carrying a tray of dirty dishes high above his head, and hurried out again with a steaming pot of coffee.

The spell was broken. Mehitabel began to speak in a trembling voice.

"Master says we're not allowed to have a funeral for Reba and Percy. He says it serves them right not to have a proper burying. Oh, mercy me." The old cook laid her head in the crook of her arm and sobbed.

"No funeral?" Cowslip gasped and jumped to her feet. "Why, their spirits can't never rest without no funeral!"

She looked from helpless face to helpless face and finally sank back into her chair. Just being ghosts was bad enough, but they had died a terrible violent way.

"Plat-eyes," she whispered. "Glory be. They're going to be plat-eyes."

"There ain't nothing we can do about it," said Hag. "The overseer done rousted out a couple of field hands before first light and sent them down to the slaves' graveyard to get the burying done."

Suddenly it was as if something deep within her had broken loose. Cowslip could no longer hold back the tears that had throbbed inside her throughout the long hours since she heard the gunshots ring out. Her face was covered with a salty wetness, and her whole body retched with each new sob. Stumbling to the back door, she raced into the morning sunshine and fell face down in the cool grass. She did not fight the wracking sobs any longer but let them break over her like waves.

She did not know how long it was before she heard the sound of footsteps and sat up. Job closed the back door quietly and hurried to her.

"Mistress will be here any minute," he said. "Colonel Sprague took the carriage into Columbus to meet her steamboat right after his breakfast. You've got to get yourself presentable."

"Job, what are we going to do?" she cried, ignoring his words completely. "Master won't allow a funeral for Reba and Percy. They'll turn to plat-eyes sure."

"You've got other things to worry about right now," he said in a soothing voice as he helped her to her feet. "You just see to it that you and the children are ready for Mistress's homecoming."

Cowslip could not understand why Job was acting this way. After all his talk about helping slaves to be free, didn't he care about Reba and Percy's poor souls? She opened her mouth to speak, but Job raised his hand for silence.

"Come to my room tonight as usual," he said. His voice had a tone of finality to it that Cowslip did not like.

A lot of good that will do, she thought angrily as she watched Job walk back toward the house.

Then she raced to catch up with him. "I almost forgot," she called. "There's something else."

"What is it?"

"There were three bodies," she said. "I saw them with my own eyes. Who was the third one?"

"His name was Roger Grayson. He was the white man I told you about who smuggled slaves up the river in his boat."

"A *white* man?" Cowslip could not believe it. "You mean a *white* man done *died* for blacks?"

"Yes, girl, he gave up his life to help Reba and Percy. He would have done the same for you."

"Me? Why would anybody, black or white, want to die for me? I ain't worth nothing to nobody."

"You're wrong," Job said calmly. "I'll bet *you* care about what happens to you."

"Sure, but what difference does that make?"

"Just that you can't say that nobody cares

about you. You are somebody, and you care about yourself. That makes you worth dying for."

Cowslip shook her head in amazement and watched Job head back toward the house.

"Then how come I feel like nobody if I'm really somebody?" she wondered.

Joel's shouts broke into her thoughts as he and Laura Margaret tumbled out the back door. "There you are. We've been looking all over for you."

"Hurry," Laura Margaret called. "Mamma's carriage is coming up the drive."

Cowslip rushed into the kitchen with the children and collected Toby, who was propped up in a chair playing with a spoon. She cleaned his hands and wiped the dribbles off his clothes and then turned to inspect Joel and Laura Margaret.

As usual, Laura Margaret was immaculate. She had chosen her very best dress for the occasion. It was a yellow muslin with a skirt that stood out like a bell over a cluster of crinoline petticoats and showed the frilly cuffs of her pantalets. It was the most grown-up dress she owned, and she smiled demurely when Cowslip nodded her approval.

Joel fidgeted uncomfortably. He hated to get dressed up, even in his sailor suit, and he toyed with the gold braid and gilt buttons, one of which dangled by a thread. Cowslip sighed a sigh of resignation, smoothed Joel's touseled hair, and steered him and Laura Margaret toward the porch.

Mistress was out of the carriage the instant it stopped, scooping Joel and Laura Margaret into her arms and hugging them so tightly that Joel squirmed to get loose. Next she ran up the porch steps to where Cowslip stood holding Toby.

"Why, he's grown so much in just a few weeks!" she exclaimed, and held out her hands to take him.

Suddenly she dropped her hands. "What is *that*?" she demanded. She was pointing at Cowslip's bell.

Cowslip looked around for Master, but he had disappeared into the house. Only Job remained, and he was busy unloading trunks from the carriage. She would have to say it out loud again. Would the shame of wearing the hateful thing never end? She dropped her eyes to the hem of Mrs. Sprague's brown silk gown and raised them inch by inch until she could face her mistress eye to eye.

"It's a bell, ma'am," Cowslip said softly. "For straying like a goat."

Slowly Mrs. Sprague pulled Toby into her

173

arms and reached out a hand to touch the rough metal of the bell. Her pale cheeks blushed deep rose, and she stared at it for a moment that seemed a whole day long to Cowslip.

Then abruptly Mrs. Sprague came to life again.

"We'll *see* about that," she said, and she snapped to attention, marching into the house with Toby's startled face bobbing over her shoulder as she went.

"What in tarnation does she mean by that?" Cowslip wondered, frowning worriedly. "I sure don't want to start no trouble."

The children swarmed around their mother most of the afternoon while she and Cowslip busied themselves unpacking. Mistress chattered happily at first, telling the children about her trip on the steamboat and about the miraculous recovery that their grandfather had made. Gradually, however, she seemed to grow annoyed with the constant clanging of Cowslip's bell. She would stop abruptly in her conversation and stare at it with an expression of both anger and disbelief.

Cowslip's heart was as heavy as her bell. It seemed certain that Mistress would not let her stay on in the big house making a racket every time she moved. She would surely be in the fields this time tomorrow.

"You may go now, Cowslip," Mistress said at last, frowning at the bell as if she were talking to it. "I want to spend the rest of the afternoon with the children. We'll finish unpacking in the morning."

Sadly, Cowslip left the room. She did not want to go down to the white cabin, where everything would remind her of Reba, so she wandered aimlessly about the big house. No one seemed to notice. Colonel Sprague was out riding over the plantation on his big black stallion attending to business matters, and the other house slaves shared the numbing grief over the death of their friends and scarcely looked up when Cowslip passed.

Finally she sat down on the steps outside the summer kitchen and looked at the honeysuckle bush that grew beside them. Underneath it was the dead bird. It had been several days since she had checked the bird, so she parted the leaves for one more look.

"Glory be," she whispered. "If that old bird ain't flatter than a flitter."

Cowslip smiled with satisfaction as a brittle feather fell away from the dried-up little body. The bird looked more like a clump of matted grass than any creature that had ever been airborne. Only the spindly legs, sticking out like twigs, and the beak, spread open by the wad of paper, gave away the fact that it had once been a bird.

"Troubles and misfortunes. Troubles and misfortunes," Cowslip sang under her breath. If anything could make her sing after what happened last night, it was the thought of what was about to happen to Master. Any day now, any minute, for all she knew, things were going to get so bad for him that he would wish he had never been so mean to his slaves. Hadn't her former master lost his whole cotton crop? That was proof enough for her that Mariah's curse would really work.

Just so long as nothing bad happens to Mistress or them young'uns, Cowslip thought, and she crossed and uncrossed her fingers three times for luck. "Troubles and misfortunes. Troubles and misfortunes," she sang.

She was still singing soundlessly to herself when she climbed through Job's window late that night.

"Are you sure no one heard you?" Job asked sternly.

"No one," she said. "House is quiet as a grave."

Job nodded. "Then follow me," he said.

An uneasy feeling settled over Cowslip as Job blew out the candle. He raised the window and slipped over the sill, reaching a hand back inside the room to help her out.

Cowslip had to run to keep up with Job's long strides as he headed straight down the hill toward the slave cabins. Wherever it was that Job was going, he wasn't wasting any time getting there. When they reached the white cabin, he slowed his pace and began to sing softly.

"O graveyard, O graveyard,
I'm walkin' through the graveyard.
Lay this body down."

Cowslip stopped dead still. She had heard that voice before. She had heard it the night Percy and the other two field hands ran away. So it had been Job singing that night as he led the field hands to the secret cave. But where was he leading her now?

Job sang so softly that Cowslip was sure no one else would hear, but as they passed each cabin the door opened and the men, women, and children who lived inside filed into the night like somber shadows. Silently they joined the single line that snaked in and out among the cabins in the moonlight.

Only once did Job stop singing — when they came near Tanner's cabin. Once they were safely past it, he began to chant again.

> "I know starlight,
> I'm walkin' through starlight,
> Lay this body down.
>
> "I know moonlight,
> I'm walkin' through moonlight,
> Lay this body down."

Where were they going? Everyone else seemed to know. The slaves were all dressed in their Sunday best, and the women carried bouquets of wild flowers. Cowslip thought of the words of the song that Job was singing. It said, "I'm walkin' through the graveyard." Was that where they were going now?

CHAPTER 18

A round full moon gleamed overhead as the long procession wound its silent way past the washhouse and into the woods like a parade of sleepwalkers.

Cowslip felt goose bumps pop out all over her arms. Even with the other slaves so near, she felt all alone and scared. If only someone would say something instead of everybody acting like dead folks.

She stumbled in the darkness and clutched at Job's sleeve to keep from falling.

"Just a little farther," he whispered. "We're almost there."

"Where?"

"Sh," he cautioned. "You mustn't make any noise."

From all sides, night birds screeched angrily at the intruders, and Cowslip wondered if the birds were trying to warn them of some danger that lay ahead. Twigs and stickers scratched her legs, and cobwebs reached down from branches high above her and clung to her face and hair.

Finally she saw the end of the woods ahead. Job's pace quickened as they neared it.

They stepped into the moonlight in a place where Cowslip had never been before. The ground they stood on was clay and table-flat. It was the top of a small bluff, with a steep, rocky drop-off to the river. Below, moonlight bobbed in the water like a school of shining fishes, and downstream a groaning barge sloshed through the inky river.

There were crosses stuck into the ground everywhere. They were not the kind of crosses found in white folks' cemeteries but were made from sticks that had been lashed together. The constant wind that blew across the bluff and the pounding of rain had caused them to jut rudely out of the ground at strange, odd angles. Most of the graves were covered with tufts of grass, but at the far end of the cemetery were three fresh mounds of dirt.

All at once Cowslip understood. Job did care after all, and now Reba's and Percy's souls could rest ... theirs and the white man's too.

"We can talk now," Job said. "Come over here and you can help me give out the torches."

Cowslip tried not to think about Mariah's ghostly warnings about graveyards after dark as she followed him to a pile of tree branches near the edge of the woods. One end of each branch was wrapped with rags.

Job pointed to a bucket that stood close by. "Dip the wrapped ends of the branches into that bucket and hand them to me," he said. "I'll light them."

Cowslip felt a wave of pride sweep over her. There had not been much that she could do to help Reba through her troubles when she was alive. At least now she had gotten to walk beside Job at the head of the procession and was helping him with the torches.

The slaves pressed around them eagerly, stretching out their hands as each dancing flame was lighted. There were not enough torches to go around, so Job picked a few of the men to bear the lights for all.

When the last torch was burning, Job held it high above his head and called Cowslip to him. The rest of the slaves fell in line behind him, spacing the torches so that the wavering light stretched out to every person.

Marching slowly toward the three fresh graves, Job began to chant again. This time his full rich tones filled the air, and one by one the others joined the song.

"O graveyard, O graveyard,
I'm walkin' through the graveyard,
Lay this body down.

"I go to judgment
In the evening of the day,
Lay this body down."

Cowslip joined in too. The song was sung often at funerals, and she knew it well. She tried to match Job's smooth deep voice with her own clear, high-pitched one, but the notes cracked and the words sounded hoarse as she fought to hold back tears.

Job led the marching slaves in a circle around the graves. The flickering light from the torches crisscrossed the mounds of dirt with eerie shadows. Finally Job stopped at the foot of the grave in the center. It was sure to be Reba's, Cowslip thought, because it was smaller than the other two.

He handed the torch to Cowslip and raised both his arms for silence. "Let us pray," he said.

There was a long pause as children were shushed and heads were bowed. Finally, Job went on. "Dear Lord, accept these humble souls. At last they've been set free. Amen."

"Amen" echoed through the crowd like distant thunder, and then all was silent again.

Slowly Mehitabel came forward, holding her bouquet of flowers out in front of her like an offering. Usually fresh graves were covered with flowers — real ones in the summer, paper ones in the winter. But surely the women wouldn't do that this time, Cowslip thought. Master might come by the cemetery and see the flower-covered graves and know that the slaves had disobeyed him and held a funeral for the runaways after all.

Cowslip watched in amazement as Mehitabel sank to her knees beside Reba's grave and dug a hole in the soft clay with her hands. Then she placed the flowers in the hole and covered them with the clay, smoothing the spot until it was impossible to tell that it had been disturbed. A few at a time, the other women came forward, and before long all three graves bore a blanket of flowers just beneath the surface of the clay.

Cowslip's heart was bursting. She had no flowers. She had no special way of saying good-bye to her friend. She looked reproachfully at Job. Why hadn't he told her what was going to happen tonight? As she turned quickly sideways to look at him, the heavy bell clanked against her chest.

The lace-edged handkerchief! Why hadn't she thought of it before? Besides, she had no right to keep it. It had been a special gift from Percy, a sign to show that he and Reba were betrothed.

Cowslip stuck the torch into the ground and went to the head of Reba's grave. She unwrapped the handkerchief from around the clapper of her bell and, kneeling, scooped a hole in the dirt and gently placed the cloth inside. Then she pulled the yellow bandanna from her head and slowly wound it around the clapper where the handkerchief had been.

The marchers were circling around the graves again. Their mournful chant rose to the sky. Cowslip did not join them this time. Instead, she sat at the head of Reba's grave gently patting the clay over the handkerchief.

It ain't right that the only way a body can

be free is to die, she thought bitterly. It ain't right, and *it ain't so*!

She looked up at the line of slaves spinning past her. They were risking their own lives to give Reba and Percy and Grayson a proper burying. Was this their way of saying that they didn't believe it either?

"Well, this ain't enough for me," Cowslip thought. "I got to do something, like Job always says I should."

Slowly she got to her feet. The marchers were moving faster and faster, and the tempo of their singing had increased with their pace. She tried to signal for them to stop and listen to her, but no one seemed to notice when she waved her arms. The slaves chanted as if they were in a trance, and Cowslip knew that, deep inside, each one was singing about his own misery and suffering as well as about the suffering of the dead. Hag, Mehitabel, even Job seemed not to see her or know that she was there.

At last, when Job passed nearby, Cowslip reached out and touched his arm. "I got something to say to everybody," she shouted, trying to make herself heard above the song.

Job nodded. "Quiet!" he cried in his commanding voice. One by one the slaves stopped marching, and a hush spread over them.

Job pushed Cowslip forward a step or two. "Go ahead," he urged. His eyes had the steady glow of stars, and the trace of a smile was on his lips as if he knew what she was going to say.

Cowslip was sure that this moment would change her life forever. She cleared her throat and looked into the sea of solemn faces.

"I swear on the grave of my friend Reba and on the grave of her man Percy and on the grave of this white man who cared enough about black folks to die for them — I swear I'm going to be *free!*"

It was as if time had stopped for an instant as the astonished slaves stared back at her. Then Job stepped forward to stand beside her, and Cowslip thought she saw a tear shining on his cheek. Job took a deep breath, closed his eyes, and began to sing.

> "No more auction block for me,
> No more, no more,
> No more auction block for me,
> Many thousand gone.

> "No more peck of corn for me,
> No more, no more,
> No more peck of corn for me,
> Many thousand gone."

Cowslip listened to the chorus of slaves sing out the words, and she remembered the night when that very song had been the signal that Percy and his companions had safely reached the river cave. She could still see the joy on Reba's face, and she now felt a joy of her own swelling up inside her as she joined in the singing.

> "No more pint of salt for me,
> No more, no more,
> No more pint of salt for me.
> Many thousand gone.

> "No more driver's lash for me,
> No more, no more,
> No more driver's lash for me,
> Many thousand gone."

The singing lasted for a long time, and then the weary slaves crept silently back to their beds. Cowslip lay awake thinking about the work she had ahead of her, the long hours with Job learning all the things that she must know to prepare herself for the step that she had chosen to take. She would miss Job and Mehitabel and Hag, and she would dearly miss the young'uns, but her mind was made up. Nothing could stop her now, no matter how long it took.

The next morning, as she brought the children down for breakfast, she heard loud, angry voices coming from the dining room.

"Master is powerful stirred up about something," said Mehitabel. A worried frown spread over her face. "Him and Mistress been going at it strong ever since they come down to breakfast."

Just then she heard Colonel Sprague call her name.

"Cowslip. Come in here."

For an instant she was frozen with fear. Did he know that she had been gone from the nursery last night? Did he know about the funeral by torchlight?

But last night she had made a vow: She was going to be free no matter what. Now she stood up tall and calmly entered the dining room.

Mistress was sitting opposite the Colonel at the big round table. There were two spots of high color on her cheeks and her eyes were blazing, but she smiled at Cowslip.

"You may go to the blacksmith and have that collar removed," the Colonel said, scowling at her.

"Yes, sir," she said. Why, Mistress had taken up for her after all!

But still, Master was in no mood to see the

gladness she felt, so she struggled to keep her expression blank. Instinctively she put a hand on the bell, and her fingers touched something soft. The yellow bandanna! She had wrapped it around the clapper last night after burying Reba's handkerchief at the grave, and she had forgotten to remove it this morning. What if the Colonel saw it? He was already angry now. What would he do if he saw that she had tried to muffle the bell?

If only one of the children would call for her from the kitchen or Toby would cry. Then maybe she could leave the dining room long enough to remove the bandanna. But the house was still.

Colonel Sprague cleared his throat loudly, breaking the silence. "Furthermore, Mrs. Sprague and I have decided to let you continue as the children's nurse."

"Yes, sir," Cowslip repeated. She was surprised at how unimportant this news seemed now.

"You're a wonder with the children," said Mistress. "We would consider it quite a misfortune to lose your services."

"Thank you," Cowslip murmured, and then she slipped quickly out of the dining room. She could scarcely hide her relief that Colonel Sprague had not seen the yellow bandanna.

She smiled to herself as she thought of Mrs. Sprague's words about how it would be a misfortune to lose her, because she was remembering her vow to be free and the dead bird drying up under the honeysuckle bush. Mariah's curse was going to work just as she had known it would.

In the kitchen Cowslip shooed Joel and Laura Margaret to the dining room to have breakfast with their parents. Then she turned to Mehitabel and asked her in words that were almost singing, "Would you mind Toby for a bit? Master done said I could go to the blacksmith and get this bell took off!"

"Mercy me, child, run on." The old cook was all smiles as she took Cowslip by the arm and hurried her toward the door.

Cowslip raced out of the house and down the hill toward the blacksmith. It did not matter now that the bell beat painfully against her chest with every step.

"Henry, Henry," she called. "Master says I don't have to wear this collar no more."

"That sure is mighty good news," said the blacksmith and he unlocked the collar and tossed it into a box full of scraps of metal and broken chains.

"Wait!" shouted Cowslip. Retrieving the collar, she unwound the yellow bandanna from around the clapper of the bell. Then,

190

with an air of scorn, she tossed the collar into the box.

She headed back up the hill toward the big house at a much slower pace than she had come down, nodding her head up and down and wiggling her shoulders, almost dizzy with lightness now that the hated collar was gone.

"I ain't never going to be belled and collared like a goat again," she thought. "I'm a human person and I got dignity."

Cowslip stopped dead still. Dignity had been Reba's word. Why had she used it now? She thought back to when Reba had said that dignity was supposed to help you not to be so scared. Hadn't she pranced into the dining room to face Master this morning with her head held high and only a little bit scared? And, she thought, if dignity meant knowing deep down that you were a human person, then once you'd worn a bell around your neck and had your friend shot dead for trying to get free, you'd know for sure that you weren't an animal and you'd get the hang of dignity right fast.

Cowslip dropped to her knees and looked at the beautiful yellow bandanna crumpled in her hand. Slowly she sat down in the grass and spread it across her lap, gently smoothing away the wrinkles.

"Job said a cowslip is a flower growing

wild and free," she whispered. She felt tingles run up and down her back as she stared at the bandanna and remembered the sound of Job's voice the first time he had spoken those words.

After a moment she tied the bandanna around her hair and stood up as tall as she could. She took a deep breath of the late-summer morning air and said out loud, "Well, then. That's what I'm going to be. A cowslip — wild and free."